THE PLOWMAN'S PLIGHT

A Carcassonne Medieval Mystery

E. A. RIVIÈRE

Cover Illustration © 100 Covers

Book Layout: David Pasquantonio

The Plowman's Plight / E. A. Rivière—1st ed.

ISBN 978-1-7372892- 하위바

For

Lovely, laughing
Eleanor,

honorable Henry,

and wise Chelsea.

All of you inspire me.

Carcassonne (now southern France), the year 1200

CHAPTER I.

Bertwoin Teisseire hid behind the damp trunks of sycamores and poplars as he crept along the lusty Aude River toward Emeline, the woodcutter's heretical daughter.

Blurred slightly by a mist swirling around her, she frolicked on the bank and stomped in puddles with girlish glee, squishing silky mud between her toes. The hems of her hooded cape, blue woolen tunic, and linen chemise slapped against her calves, and a reed basket hanging from her arm bounced against her bony hip.

Bertwoin tiptoed to within three paces of her without being seen or heard. Emeline began singing a troubadour's lament. Enchanted, he watched her coltish capering and listened to her silver-pure voice. Anyone would envy her primitive joy.

Grinning, he asked, "Does your prancing cause toadstools to jump into your basket?"

Startled, she whirled and reached under her cape for the knife hanging on her braided belt. Then she recognized Bertwoin, hopped a few more defiant steps, and put her hands on her waist. "I am *not* a witch."

"Ah, I'd not accuse you of such. But even charms chanted by ordinary folk sometimes work."

Emeline smirked at the broken scythe handle Bertwoin carried. Both pieces slanted against his left shoulder, which was twisted slightly higher than his other one, the mark of an experienced plowman.

Emeline sang,

> *"A plowman named Ox,*
> *proved too strong for his tool,*
> *so he sought a charm to mend it,*
> *to escape from men's ridicule."*

Bertwoin didn't take insult at her calling him Ox...far from it. The nickname praised his manly strength, and oxen were useful beasts, especially for heavy plowing in the marshlands. They also had fewer sins than, say, wily pigs or the balky mules that pulled his swing plow.

Not wanting, however, to fall mightily into the sin of pride, he confessed, "It wasn't my strength that snapped this handle in two, Cricket. The wood dried out and weakened. It broke when the blade struck a stone. And I'll not need a charm to mend it. I'm on my way to see my Uncle Roland. He'll either repair the handle or make me another one."

Emeline made a chucking sound with her tongue. "Cricket, am I?"

"Did I not see you hopping about like one? And do you not chirp love songs?" Bertwoin jerked his chin at the reed basket she carried. "Toadstools?"

She sang,

> *"I need herbs to spice my potage,*
> *and whatever else comes to hand,*
> *so I hunt hidden thyme and ripe berries,*
> *and forage the wide, wooded land."*

Bertwoin clapped. "You should entertain at the *visconte's* feasts. His guests will toss you silver coins to hear you sing about my tool."

She curtsied. "You flatter me. You'll be at the harvest *fete*, will you not?"

He smiled down at her mud-caked feet. "Only if you are there to dance with me."

She ducked her head in the calculated pose of a shy maiden. "And why would you *ever* want to dance with me?"

"To make Sebastian and all of the other fellows jealous. Why else?"

Born a year before the Third Crusade, Emeline was nearly fourteen years old. Not yet married to Sebastian Rives, a fletcher, she soon would be, unless his brother, Villenc, prevented the wedding. He raged against her Good Folk beliefs.

She cocked her head to one side and smiled up at Bertwoin. "I might let the dancer who pleases me most kiss me."

"Well then, I will practice my dancing. *And* my kissing."

"On Rixende?"

He dodged the trap of talking about Rixende, a buxom girl who had infatuated him, and bragged, "If you kiss me once, you'll want a second one."

Pretending to be shocked, she laid a hand over her breasts. "And I had always believed oxen were humble beasts."

Bertwoin squinted into the mist behind her and sighed. "But not all fellows dance, do they?"

Two monks scuffled toward them, their arms crossed over

3

their bellies, their hands tucked into the opposite sleeves of their black robes. Brother Gregorius, blond as wheat and also tall enough to look Bertwoin directly in the eye, strode along beside Brother Nigellus, who was not more than a hand's width taller than Emeline and had skin the color of a ripe acorn. They were often seen together, which was as surprising as a stoat keeping company with a fox. They were alike, though, in the fact that their humility was mere pretense.

Emeline groaned and whispered, "Brother Nigellus follows me like a wart on my butt."

"Does his interest not flatter you?" Bertwoin teased.

Had Emeline truly been a witch, her damning glance would have turned him into a heron's hopping dinner.

The monks halted, their coarse habits smelling of incense even though the cleansing drizzle had soaked them. Brother Nigellus cast sly glances at Emeline, while Brother Gregorius made a pious point of ignoring her.

Emeline feigned a smile of welcome and said, "God grant you peace."

"And may the *true* faith grant you peace," Brother Nigellus muttered.

Emeline smiled sweetly. "It does."

Bertwoin hid his amusement behind a polite expression. Everyone in the diocese knew that Brother Nigellus had made it his mission to rid Emeline of her belief in the Good Folk's teachings. He had donned this duty like a cilice, the sackcloth shirt worn to mortify the flesh.

Brother Nigellus cleared his throat. "Have you thought further about my lecture on the first commandment?"

She glanced slyly at Bertwoin before answering the monk with practiced bashfulness, "I remember your sermon well, brother, and think of little else."

Emeline was fractious and would suffer a beating rather than submit. A monk had told Bertwoin that Emeline's polite but stubborn resistance often caused Brother Nigellus to pray with gritted teeth for Saint Nazarius to give him patience.

"She is lucky," Bertwoin quipped, "to receive so much of your attention."

Brother Nigellus studied his expression before he shrugged. "It is my duty."

Bertwoin had heard that this monk's duty was often more of a burden to others than to himself. Though he walked with studied humility, a wolfish aura of priestly ambition clung to him. His detractors said his true religion was power, and that through cunning and flattery rather than prayer and self-denial, he hoped to become an abbot.

In contrast, Brother Gregorius had chosen a path that had earned him the nickname, "the saint." He desired martyrdom. The priest of Bourg, one of the villages huddled below the high-walled citadel of Carcassonne, sometimes compared Brother Gregorius's dreams to those found in the Book of Revelation.

Bertwoin glanced at the monk's drawn face. How could he not fear sleep when haunted by such horrific visions?

"It is a blessing when one's duty furthers the will of God," Bertwoin told Brother Nigellus.

"There is no higher calling."

Emeline cleared her throat. "But how can one be certain they know the will of God?"

"The Bible teaches us this," Brother Nigellus said. "And we have the example of Jesus's life."

Emeline frowned. "If I knew God's will, I fear I would fall into the sin of pride."

Brother Nigellus shook his head. "God protects those who have true faith."

"And rewards those who are humble," Bertwoin added. He looked at the little monk with his arms crossed over his plump belly. "I hear fasting also pleases the Holy Spirit and might be rewarded with a vision."

Brother Nigellus made the sign of the cross. "May it be so."

Bertwoin smiled to hide his contempt. The little monk was said to be overly fond of peacock meat spiced with pepper, cinnamon, and cloves. He was also said to drink double his share of the abbey's sour wine or dark beer. Brother Gregorius, of course, was emaciated from constant fasting.

"And chastity," Emeline added. To guard her virginity, she took care to never be alone with Brother Nigellus.

Emeline thrust her head forward, her eyes on the monk's hand. "You're wounded."

He shrugged away her concern. "Aah, a few scratches."

So the story was true. Brother Nigellus *had* caught a black cat he claimed was the familiar of a Good Folk witch. He *had* hung the cat, its claws scrabbling at air, from his rope belt.

Brother Gregorius stared upriver with a bored expression. He was known to flagellate himself until he fainted from pain and loss of blood. He would then lie unconscious on the limestone floor of his cell until a novice sent to fetch him found him. Gregorius meant to bleed his way into heaven. So said Brother Theodoric, the abbey's infirmarian, who often complained of the never-ending burden of preparing woundwort salves to heal the inflamed lacerations crisscrossing the young saint's back.

Bertwoin frowned at someone on the misty riverbank behind the monks. "Oh, here comes Tolarto." His afternoon suddenly seemed crowded with unwelcome men. "He owes me a debt."

Tolarto dodged into the wavering shadows and drizzle drifting between the trees.

Bertwoin laughed. "Ah, he's seen me."

Brother Gregorius muttered, "Another heretic."

Brother Nigellus twitched his head to one side. "But Tolarto's belief in their teachings is weak." He glared at Emeline. "Not like this one's betrayal of our faith."

Bertwoin continued to stare at the spot where Tolarto had entered the forest. Why was the muleteer not at work? There was nothing in these hushed woods for him, unless he had come to visit the charcoal makers.

Bertwoin sniffed the air and savored the fragrant scent of burning wood. Like Emeline's woodcutter father, the charcoalers worked hidden away in the woods, and so, many people believed they knew dark secrets and practiced devilish ways.

But Tolarto was more likely to steal charcoal than to buy it. He would have no luck against these men. They kept vigil over their fire day and night.

Bertwoin moved both pieces of the broken scythe handle to his right shoulder. "Let me see if I can catch the rogue before I visit my uncle."

To give Emeline an excuse to escape from the bothersome monks, he pointed an elbow at the wet forest and told her, "You'll need to get on with gathering your toadstools, Cricket, if you don't want nightfall to catch you. God grant all of you peace." Bertwoin strode around the monks.

"As he said," Emeline told the frowning monks, "I must hurry off to pick blackberries and mushrooms."

"Your soul, girl, is more important than the fruits of the forest," Brother Nigellus scolded. "You risk damnation."

EMELINE WANTED TO ASK ABOUT HIS SOUL AND TO REMIND him that lust and gluttony were deadly sins. But arguing with

Brother Nigellus would only prolong her time in his sanctimonious presence.

"I guard both my soul and my body," she said and fled into the forest before Brother Nigellus could grab her arm.

"We must talk," he called.

She wiggled her fingers over her shoulder in farewell without looking back.

"I'll not be denied," he yelled.

Emeline lifted her face to the cold drizzle. Gertrude had said a gentle mist put the bloom of a rose petal on a young woman's cheek. She smiled at the thought of kissing Bertwoin. She would make certain he danced with her.

The forest darkened, and its silence deepened as Emeline moved away from the river's hiss. She threaded her way through the underbrush toward a tangled patch of blackberry bushes, searching for green herbs to pick along the way. She just had time to pick the ripe berries and hurry home.

She adored the woods when they lay quiet and mysterious like this. This mist would cause mushrooms to sprout overnight. She must remember to gather them tomorrow while the morning was still newborn.

Emeline found a cluster of honeycomb morels and stooped to pick them. Her father loved them fried in lard. And Sebastian was coming to eat at their house tomorrow. A cook at the *Chateau Comtal* had given her father rosemary and tarragon "under the table." She also had pomegranate juice and ground almonds. With these and the morels, she would show Sebastian she could cook a delicious capon dinner. She would be a wife worth having.

She frowned at the thought of Villenc, Sebastian's younger brother. He was a stonebreaker, well-muscled, and a good worker, but he raged against her Good Folk beliefs. He had warned Sebastian that if they married, he would stab her eyes out with his chisel.

She sighed. Bertwoin had been born the year Pope Alexander III died, and she the year before the Third Crusade, so he was maybe five years older. It was a shame he was not yet settled enough to take a wife. He had the steady nature of an ox and probably wouldn't beat her unless she deserved it.

Of course, if she were to marry him, she would have to live in his father's *ostal*. Would Bertwoin be strong enough to protect her from grim Clanoud? Or worse, as he grew older, would Bertwoin become like his father?

Emeline jerked as if coming awake. A large shadow had slipped behind a nearby tree in the hushed, somber woods. Gooseflesh dimpled her upper arms. Emeline rested her hand on her knife handle and scanned the dripping foliage.

The Devil's Doorstep was only a short walk from where she now stood. Did its evil reach this far? Was the ghost of a hanged criminal or a roving demon stalking her? She stopped and heard nothing other than the patter of drops rolling off high leaves and smacking lower ones.

Let it not be a demon, she prayed. *Saint Mary Magdalene, preserve me from harm.*

Then she heard rustling behind her. Not a ghost, then, because they made no noise. Was it a squirrel or a roving pig? No, something inside her sensed leprous evil.

Emeline took slow, deep breaths to control her impulse to flee. She began to hum a tune. Knowing she must not go deeper into the dark forest, she sauntered toward the Aude river.

Something shifted in the murky underbrush twenty paces in front of her. She angled farther left and walked faster.

Please, Saint Mary Magdalene, if it is not an animal, turn it into one.

She must reach the river. People were there—fishermen, boatmen, or pilgrims. She wanted to throw away her basket and run, but that might provoke it to attack her. Better to let it stalk her while she moved ever closer to the Aude.

Was it someone playing a joke on her…Bertwoin? *Please let it be*. Maybe Brother Nigellus was punishing her.

She sidestepped around a thick, towering maple, its canopy drooping with water. A strong hand clamped over her mouth and snapped her head backward. She screamed, but her cry was too muffled for anyone on the riverbank to hear her.

She flailed about, struggling to free herself. Her attacker jerked her against his hard body. She tried to bite the palm of the cold hand clamped over her mouth. Her elbow struck his ribs. He huffed and snarled and lifted her off her feet.

A woolen sleeve scraped across her throat, and his forearm tightened, choking her. Tiny comets whirled in front of her eyes. She remembered her knife and fumbled for it, but her numb fingers had no strength in them. Her legs jittered. The forest darkened as if she were falling into a deep well.

CHAPTER II.

Clanoud sat like an emperor on an oak stump under the spreading limbs of a mighty elm outside their house. Bertwoin watched his father slide a close-grained whetstone along a curved scythe blade. They listened to it sing its sharpness with only two scratchy notes.

A sly, catlike smile crimped Clanoud's thin lips, and his eyes glowed with haughty amusement. He had waited days for this.

Bertwoin surveyed their land and cottage as he considered how he should bring up his problem.

The peasant families around the windswept village of Montredon plowed three fields in common and seeded them with hemp, barley, wheat, oats, and rye. They worked one field in spring, another in fall, and one was left to rest for a year to regain its black-dirt vigor.

Bertwoin had plowed six squares for Tolarto Malet, a farmer and muleteer who had been flogged twice for idleness. That was in spring, and the summer harvest was now done, yet Bertwoin still couldn't get the lumbering bastard to pay him their agreed-upon price, one suckling pig.

Bertwoin huffed in defeat. "You ever have any trouble getting somebody to pay you?"

Clanoud frowned a moment, as if shocked by the idea that his son would think anyone would refuse to pay him. "I had some problems when I was still a pup and finding my own way, but they soon died off. Everybody came to understand that I get what's coming to me and mine. You got a problem?" he asked, as if he didn't know that Tolarto owed his eldest son, and therefore his own household, a piglet.

Clanoud again slid the honing stone down the length of his scythe blade with his eyes closed as he felt for tiny hesitations in the stone's smooth glide.

"Ah, a small one," Bertwoin said.

"There ain't no *small* when it comes to being owed. If you let that whoreson cheat you out of a single egg, he and others like him will steal six eggs off you next time." Clanoud set the whetstone beside him on the stump and rubbed his gnarly hands together, clearly enjoying their conversation.

Bertwoin stared at the ground. Few things delighted his father more than bloodying noses or breaking fingers, especially when he was justified in doing so. In this case, anybody could see that Tolarto was spitting on the honor of their *ostal*.

Though his father was only of medium height, when he fought, demonic rage possessed him and numbed him to both pain and mercy. This allowed him to overwhelm larger men. He was always ready to use his fists and pulp someone's lips or use his keen knife to gut-cut a belly, if it came to that. He had killed two men since returning from the Holy Land and maimed another, all done in self-defense, of course. The one he had maimed only lived because three other men and one courageous woman had pulled his father, squalling and snarling, to the ground and smothered his fury.

Like a veteran tomcat, his lean body carried numerous battle scars: puckered knife cuts, the half-blind squint of his left eye, the discolored slash from a Saracen's sword across his left thigh, and the tip of a little finger chopped off in an alehouse brawl. His crooked nose whistled when he took a slow, deep breath. Blows and bites had disfigured his ears until they resembled ragged fungi clinging to an oak's trunk. He limped, sometimes pissed in his bed at night, and his speech was often slurred.

Bertwoin had to admit, though, that their family benefited from his father's temper. Dishonest people either avoided members of his household or became temporarily honest when doing business with them. Which made what Tolarto had done surprisingly stupid.

Clanoud cleared his throat. "I warned you to stay away from that useless dog turd. Why would you ever hire out to him? He'd cut the wings off an angel and sell the feathers as charms."

Clanoud rapped Bertwoin's shin with the hickory handle of his scythe. Bertwoin hopped out of range on one foot and tried to rub the hurt out of his lower leg.

"Tricked his eldest daughter out of her rightful dowry, didn't he?" Clanoud continued. "And his two sons are little better than he is. Which is why every day their family sinks deeper into the muck. The mother's the only one whose tongue isn't twisted out of shape by black lies."

Bertwoin hadn't reckoned on Tolarto not paying him, or that he would brag at Tisbe's alehouse of tricking Clanoud's stupid eldest son into breaking ground for him for free. It's almost as if he wanted a beating. No doubt, people in the village waited to see how Bertwoin, and his relentless father, would settle the debt Tolarto owed them.

Clanoud took a swipe with his scythe at a nearby weed and cut off its tuft. "You used *my* mules to plow his sections. Hah, I might be able to go to the council about it, even without two witnesses. Everybody and their green-eyed cat knows you didn't plow his land for free."

He glowered at Bertwoin and continued, "I still haven't heard why you scratched out furrows for that sore on a fat bishop's ass. Or why you waited a whole season before you decided to force him to pay you."

Bertwoin had cut the furrows so Aalis, Tolarto's suffering wife, would have more than chaff to feed her family come autumn and early winter. Tolarto wasn't going to get the plowing done, was he? Or at least not in time for a plentiful harvest.

Bertwoin shrugged. "His family's got to eat."

His father took a vicious swipe at another clump of weeds. "Left and Right have more common sense than you do," he said, naming the two mules that pulled their swing plow.

"I can take care of this." They both knew he had asked for his father's advice because he couldn't handle the problem on his own.

Clanoud pointed at where they threw scraps to their pigs. "I'm not seeing a new squealer where it should be." He scowled at Bertwoin. "You do know that if I ever thought I was raising a halfwit or a coward, I'd smother you and feed your corpse to the pigs. Someday you'll take a wife."

Bertwoin remembered Emeline's promise of a kiss.

"Might be by then," his father said. "I won't be here to wipe your ass every time you fart wrong. You'll need to care for her and your mother and any of your unmarried sisters. You'll need the respect of our neighbors."

"I'll get it."

"Not if you act squirrelly." Clanoud sat up straighter. "Family and reputation are all that keep us safe. The Church and nobility and even the Good Folk who claim to walk in the footsteps of the poor Apostles leech away our work and our food. They're all clawing at us."

"I stand up for myself when I have to," Bertwoin muttered. Though he didn't enjoy eye-gouging and smacking noses, he knew he had to keep the reputation of someone who didn't walk away from a quarrel. Muscling a swing plow all day had put strength in his body. Now all he needed was the willingness to fight.

"I'll not let the honor of our house turn to ash, boy," Clanoud grumbled. "How can I look my brother or anyone else in the eye if I do?"

Bertwoin kept his face as bland as a flat puddle. His Uncle Laurence, a bachelor who lived with them, used words, not fists, to defend their family. "Tolarto claims he already paid me."

"Well now, that's a problem with hair on it, ain't it? All because you were too pigheaded to listen to me. You should never have worked for that mangy cur. Weak men like him draw strength off stronger men and women."

CHAPTER III

Clanoud seemed to have tossed the festering problem of Tolarto cheating his son in a bucket and put a lid on it. So Bertwoin waited. Ignoring something was not the same as forgetting it. His father was too rooster-proud of his reputation as a prosperous farmer and ex-crusader to let any insult pass.

Therefore, when his father told him to put on his leather boots so he could carry turnips to the Sunday market, work usually done by his *maman* and sisters, Bertwoin knew to expect trouble. Thus he wasn't overly surprised when after mass, they shoved their way through the busy market crowd that yelled and laughed and bargained for bread, vegetables, eggs, and poultry. His father found Tolarto's wife sitting on the ground behind a basket of goose eggs. They watched her sell four of them to a wool merchant's red-haired slave.

Bertwoin looked everywhere but down at Aalis, a woman who suffered the torments of Job's wife because her family had given her in marriage to a worthless rascal. Bertwoin now wished he had handled this himself. No matter how this turned out, Aalis was going to suffer because of her husband's stupidity.

"I've got good eggs here, Clanoud," she said, not quite looking him in the eye. She knew, of course, that a farmer like Clanoud had plenty of goose eggs of his own. The poor woman was frantically trying to keep Clanoud from maiming her husband.

Tolarto and his two scruffy boys, two future wife-beaters, stood nearby. They looked as if a wheel had just fallen off their cart, and they had no idea how they were going to put it back on.

Tolarto pulled out his knife and began cleaning his dirty fingernails. His woolen tunic, as usual, looked as if he had stripped it off a beggar, but his sandals were new. Bertwoin doubted he had paid anyone for them. Aalis and her two boys, of course, were barefoot and wore undyed tunics that had been patched several times.

Had the Malets already eaten the suckling pig they owed him? Along with his wife and two sons, Tolarto lived with a shepherd, a lame sister who was the shepherd's mistress, and his mother. Though no real illness afflicted the mother, most days she lay on a thin mattress of hay in her private room. A scold, she might demand that her doting son feed her the suckling pig. Its soft meat would give her the strength to live.

Tolarto's two boys stood tall, their arms crossed over their chests, trying to look indomitable. But like their mother, their eyes never met Clanoud's.

"I understand you owe a debt to my simple-minded boy here," Clanoud said.

Tolarto yawned. "That's news to me."

Sensing drama, people began to gather around them, forming a hushed spot in the clamorous market. A nut vendor near them stopped shouting that his early-season almonds would put vigor in a man's sex life.

Most of the crowd around them, it was clear to Bertwoin, sided with his father, the ex-crusader who was a shrewd bargainer but mostly honest in his dealings. Tolarto glanced around like a cornered mouse. Everyone waited, knowing Clanoud fought like an enraged cock and broke bones. The muleteer, though, looked burly enough to make the fight entertaining.

Clanoud frowned down at the goose eggs, and Aalis put a protective hand over them. The coins and barter she got from the eggs at the market each week fed her family until their harvested wheat and rye were threshed and milled.

"He plowed your share of the field," Clanoud told Tolarto. "Only the blind didn't see him do it. We'll take what profit the eggs bring you today as payment."

The muleteer snorted. "I already paid him once and don't intend to do it twice. If he says different, then he's, uh, forgotten that I paid him. That's the way of it."

Though Tolarto was only half as clever as a chicken, he knew better than to call Bertwoin a liar, and thus, insult his father's raising of him.

Clanoud's joyless chuckle ridiculed the lie. "And you'll swear an oath on your head that you paid him?"

The muleteer reared back. "Don't need to. My plain word rings like gold."

Bertwoin muttered, "Your lies weigh you down like lead."

Tolarto now found it to his advantage to honor the Good Folks' teaching against swearing oaths. After all, he didn't want to put his soul in danger. He had, though, conveniently ignored the fact that the Good Folk were called "those who do not lie." Many of them even refused to lie to a tribunal when accused of preaching heresy.

Tolarto pointed his knife at Bertwoin's face. "Don't insult me, young pup."

Clanoud sneered at the knife. Tolarto seemed surprised to

find it in his hand. He shoved it back in the leather sheath on his rope belt. If this argument ended as a fight, knives were best left out of it.

"I ain't seen any payment," Clanoud said.

Bertwoin stepped over to Tolarto's eldest son and stared down into his freckled, sun-tanned face. The boy's grin faded.

After all, Bertwoin was Clanoud's son. When he was no more than twelve, a half-grown boar had threatened his sister, Rachel, while they were gathering firewood in the forest. Bertwoin had pulled his knife and stepped in front of Rachel when the boar charged them. The rangy pig had savaged him until he'd finally sliced open its throat. Clanoud had carried his son's bloody body home for his wife, Ellyn, to sew up and nurse back to health.

The local folk, hearing of young Bertwoin's feat, had shrugged at the time and said, "What do you expect? A pear tree begets pear trees, an oak more oaks. In a fight, Bertwoin will show out like his father."

Tolarto now nodded, as if they had reached an agreement. "Maybe he didn't give it to you. But I gave him a suckling pig. Just looking at it, you could almost taste its sweet meat. And Aalis gave him a cabbage or two from the croft to go with it."

Bertwoin spat on the ground, but before he could argue, Clanoud pointed at his face. "Did you set that suckling pig to a sow somewhere to let her raise it to full growth?"

Aalis said, "Maybe it's still with us. Bertwoin needs to come fetch it."

Clanoud nodded. "That might be the way of it."

Bertwoin waited for Tolarto to apologize and sidestep their quarrel.

"No." The muleteer crossed his arms across his chest. He jerked his chin stiff with a tuft of greasy beard at Bertwoin. "I saw him walk off with it under his arm."

Bertwoin groaned. Even a cantankerous mule would have taken the easy path Aalis had laid out for it.

Smiling, Clanoud shook an accusing forefinger at Bertwoin's chest. "Maybe the suckling pig ate the cabbages, and then you feasted on the porker alone."

A few people in the eager crowd laughed, others grinned.

Bertwoin tapped his forehead. "Now I remember. *Maman* cooked it for me. We forgot to give you any. But we did invite *Visconte* Raimon-Rogièr to our feast. He's fond of suckling pig."

Someone shouted, "Did you sit at high table with him?"

"No, he graced our table."

"Was it to his taste?"

"It was well salted," Bertwoin called back, as if they could afford expensive seasonings.

"He probably gave the pig to a whore," Tolarto said with a malicious grin.

Clanoud half-closed his eyes. "He's been brought up to take care of his family, which is more than can be said of a mule's ass like you. He doesn't lie. I know there never was a pig given in payment."

"You calling me a liar?" Tolarto growled.

In the sudden quiet around them, Bertwoin heard a blue tit cheep in a nearby tree. He faced Tolarto's sons, prepared to fight.

"Liar?" Clanoud muttered. "Calling a leper's pustule like you a liar would be a compliment. Calling you an ass-crack would be a compliment. An ass has a purpose. You don't."

"The suckling's still at our house." Aalis stared down at the goose eggs in her reed basket. Then she raised her face like a martyr in the desert and gazed up into Tolarto's blazing fury.

"I'll take the beating," she told him. "Better that than

watch my boys get hurt because you won't pay your debts like one of the true faith."

"Well," he sneered, "we'll see what's waiting for you when you get home, woman."

"Keep the pig."

Shocked, everyone turned toward Bertwoin. "You need it more than we do."

Clanoud stared at him a moment with his mouth open, then growled, "Hold your mouth, boy."

Aalis nodded at Bertwoin, thanking him silently, but then she shook her head. "That was kindly done, Bertwoin, and marks you as generous Christian. But it would be a sin for us to prosper by doing wrong."

"By God," Tolarto shouted, "I'll pay the debt twice over before I take charity from you."

Bertwoin stepped closer to stand nose-to-nose with him. "You're not paying the debt twice, and everybody here knows it. You lie like a priest selling fake relics. May crows feed on your eyes."

Aalis said, "We're paying, and that's the end of it. Fresh eggs!" she shouted to the crowd. "Fresh eggs for sale here. Took them out from under the geese this very morning."

Clanoud told Tolarto, "It's your debt. So you or one of your boys will bring the pig and cabbages to our farm. Today."

Then he turned and pushed through the disappointed throng. Bertwoin, relieved Tolarto hadn't punched him in a crazy moment of anger, followed his father.

It was a wet day, and birds flew over them as if they were swimming under the low clouds. On the dirt road leading out of Bourg, Clanoud clapped his hands once. "Your public offer of charity was a belly blow to him. You shamed Tolarto good."

"I was trying to save Aalis from a beating."

"That's beyond your doing, boy. She may have saved him

from getting his nose broken, but she also went against him." Clanoud rubbed his hands together. "Speaking of blows, it would have been a grand fight. You'd have taken his two boys like a fox taking hens."

His father frowned at him. "Had your charity been accepted, though, I would have kicked your ass from Bourg's gate all the way home. I'm not sure yet whether you're stupid as a stump or smarter than a ripe old fox."

Bertwoin wanted to believe that if his father had tried to beat him in public, he would have given the market crowd the fight they longed to see. But he might not have fought back.

Clanoud looked far into the distance beyond the vineyards and fields of grain at gray mountains stretched along the eastern horizon. "Lord, 'tis a fine day."

"For us," Bertwoin muttered. "What man would bruise his wife with his fists for the insult of protecting him?"

"What did she expect? She gainsaid him." Clanoud grunted. "But he might wake up one morning with a new smile under his chin." He drew a finger across his throat. "She's got grown sons now to farm for her, and they've been on the wrong end of Tolarto's fists too often to grieve his dying."

Clanoud smiled at his thoughts, then winked at Bertwoin. "Aalis also has got you to plow for her when need be, you being such a good Christian and given to being overly compassionate toward other folks."

He rubbed two fingers against his thumb, making the sign for money. "Well, I think we'll just let this new piglet of ours grow to foraging size. Or we could sell it now to the *chateau* steward. You might see a coin in profit after you pay me for the mules you used when you cut dirt for Tolarto."

He grinned up at the rain clouds. "Well, this has been a blessed morning, even without the sport of breaking Tolarto's nose for him." Then he squinted down the rutted road. "Isn't that your friend, Michel Azema, the shepherd?"

A young man in a tattered tunic waved to them before he slipped like a whisper into the forest.

Clanoud backhanded Bertwoin's upper arm. "I thought he was hiding in a high mountain pasture somewhere. What's he doing here? The *bayle* will know he's come home within a day or two."

Bertwoin shrugged. Only two nights before, he had sneaked Michel into the abbey to sell Brother Theodoric a bag of seeds. "Michel is one fox who'll run the *bayle* in circles."

They crossed a wide, rutted road that led to the main wooden bridge over the Aude and continued on a narrow road toward their hamlet of Montredon. Not long afterward, Clanoud veered onto a half-hidden footpath that most people, except him, avoided even during daylight. It was the shortest route to their *ostal*.

In the time it would take to plow four long furrows, they came within sight of the Devil's Doorstep, a crossroads overshadowed by a massive patriarchal tree called the Gallows Oak. Bourg, of course, had a permanent gallows set up in its main square, but both the bishop and *visconte* preferred to use this tree to rid the world of criminals. It stood deep in the pagan woods, and this dramatized the fact that the souls choked out of the criminals hung on the Gallows Oak were going directly to Hell.

Today at least, no putrefying bodies dangled at the ends of braided hemp ropes. Many believed that when a man or a woman was hanged, some of their life force seeped into the rope. Ugly Thea, a local wise woman, collected them after the rotting corpses had dropped off. She burned the ropes and stirred their ashes into lamb broths. Her dead man's soup was said to cure diseases of the throat.

Bertwoin coughed, the noise loud in the funereal quiet. His father hissed for him to stay silent.

Two magpies sat on a sturdy oak limb, waiting for a feast of eyes and entrails. Clanoud made the sign of the cross over his chest. "One for sickness, two for death. A bad omen." He laid a hand on the hilt of his dagger as if he would fight Death Itself if It dared to hinder his march home.

Bertwoin felt the back of his neck prickle and also made the sign of the cross. "God protect us."

After dark, only witches dared come to the Devil's Doorstep. It was said they gained power by dancing with the dead or demons.

When they reached the crossing paths under the Gallows Oak, they saw Flowia, the alchemist's virgin, strolling toward them.

"Another bad omen," Clanoud muttered.

Bertwoin hoped his father didn't embarrass him. Dark-eyed Flowia had her long black hair tucked behind her head in a white linen coif. Her heart-shaped face was the color of tanned leather. His father believed she was tainted with Moorish blood and held her accountable for her ancestry. His Uncle Laurence despised her heritage even more so than his father did.

Bertwoin's groin tightened as he watched Flowia saunter toward them, the bottom of her dress swishing from side to side over goat-skin shoes with wooden soles. She rarely wore a tunic. His father judged this as her way of showing that she was better than the peasants and took her arrogance as a personal insult.

She greeted them and asked, "Have you seen Emeline?"

"The woodcutter's daughter?" Bertwoin asked. "I saw her yesterday. She was gathering mushrooms and berries not far from the *visconte's* mill."

Flowia looked him boldly in the eye, and he averted his

gaze. It was rumored she could bewitch a man, then barter away his soul to the Devil. He didn't believe this, of course, but it was better to be safe. She did have power. He felt it in the deep well of his stomach.

"She has not returned home," Flowia told them.

Bertwoin remembered petite Emeline laughing up into his face. A chilling premonition told him she would not dance with him at the *fete*.

Clanoud laid a hand on his dagger's hilt and looked down the empty path behind them. "Death attends this spot. It's best not to mention her name and have Death mark her for Its grim harvest."

Flowia put a hand over her mouth to hide her smile. "Well, if you hear any word of Emeline before Death does, be sure to relate it to Agbart. He's searching under cabbage leaves for her."

Clanoud crowded closer to her. "You've had no father to teach you manners. And even a beggar wouldn't marry you, so you've no husband either. But if need be, I'm willing to teach you respect if the alchemist neglects his duty."

Flowia glared up into his face, almost daring him to hit her.

Bertwoin said quickly, "*Papa*, it's just her manner."

Though no one could name or number the alchemist's true powers, everyone knew he possessed some. And Bert-woin doubted the master would take kindly to anyone hitting his virgin. She was said to be necessary for his magic.

"Then maybe she needs to change her manner." One side of Clanoud's mouth curled with contempt. "It's no surprise to meet her at the Devil's Doorstep, is it? Putting a dress on a sow doesn't change it from being a muck-loving pig. And you don't need to take her side in this matter, boy." He flicked his fingers at a small clay pot she carried. "She's probably carrying a love potion to take advantage of some poor servant girl's dream, or maybe it's a poison paste for ridding a faithless hag of her husband. That's the true manner of her sort."

Flowia snorted and shoved her pot toward him. "Smell it."

Clanoud backed away. "I'll not snuffle a witch's potion."

"Gertrude just lost her middle daughter to the spitting-blood sickness," she muttered. "She requested my rose ointment for the girl's corpse." Flowia sniffed, her contempt blunt as a cudgel. "You accuse me of witchery. Based on what? The gossip of idle old men? They're nothing more than drooling simpletons."

Clanoud clenched his hands into fists. "I'm not a silly old gossip."

Flowia stood proud as a princess. "And I'm not a witch. If I were, I'd send you dancing to Hell. And I don't like being accused of taking advantage of women in need. Not when I heal them and help prepare their children's bodies for burial."

"We all have our duties," Clanoud said dismissively.

"Yes, and you once had the duty of ridding many mothers of their sons."

"I fought your people for the true faith."

"They weren't my people. And you fought for glory, not faith."

"Glory in Heaven."

Flowia ended the argument by turning away from Clanoud to inspect Bertwoin, as if measuring him and his mood. Again he averted his gaze, though he watched her from the corner of his eye. Her manner regal, she strode around them and headed in the direction of Gertrude's house.

CHAPTER IV.

O n a morning when the Dog Star was ascendant, a fisherman named Janus Lizier hooked the most dangerous catch of his long life.

The sun had just crested the mountain range stretched along the far horizon. As he crept to the water's edge so as not to scare away any fish, he saw a white lump bobbing on the river's acorn-brown surface. He pulled his cloak tighter around his scrawny neck and glanced behind him at the citadel placed like a radiant, golden crown on its hill. If no one stole this corpse from him, he would earn the finder's fee. Silver coins would clink in his purse. At the tavern, ale would flow for him as if gushing from a fountain.

The white was a linen chemise clinging wetly to a slim body floating face down in the water. The dark-brown hair spread across her back reached to her waist. Her body had snagged on a downed willow, a favorite feeding place for perch.

The young woman's gown was ripped, and its ragged hem blackened by fire. Was she a stranger, or was this the corpse of a daughter or wife he would recognize when he rolled her over?

Janus sniffed at the faint burnt-wood smell in the air. Did she belong with the charcoalers? Had her dress accidentally caught fire at their kiln?

He glanced up at the cloudless sky and thanked God for this bountiful find. Now he must hurry. He uncoiled a nettle-hemp throwing line with an iron hook already tied to its end.

Guillaume Maurs, the drowned-finder, had not yet discovered her. Janus whispered thanks to Saint Anthony. The corpse belonged to him alone. If he reached the *bayle* first and led him to this body, he would earn the finder's fee. Of course, to keep peace with the knavish Guillaume, he would have to share out a coin or two.

Guillaume and his two oafish sons were not men you angered. Whispers said that when business was slow, they sometimes drowned a beggar or two for the fees. They were also not above robbing and drowning a solitary pilgrim or peasant woman on her way to a town market.

Even the *bayle*, who worked for the *visconte's* seneschal and who had traveled on the Third Crusade with King Philip II, stayed clear of them. If he could catch the three of them murdering a beggar, he would arrest them all and make certain they never left the dungeon except to hang. But Guillaume and his sons were careful to commit their crimes alone. Two of them always stayed away to avenge any lawful justice brought against the murderer.

Janus flicked his line with practiced skill over the floating body and pulled the barbed hook toward him until it caught on the corpse's floating arm. He jerked his braided line to set the hook in her flesh and began pulling the slim body wobbling on the thick water toward the bank.

The corpse caught on one of the downed willow's limbs. He tried to pull it free. The thin arm rose as if pointing a hand at him. Janus crossed himself and jerked harder. The hook ripped free.

"Devil take you," he growled, not stuttering because he never did when talking to himself.

He pulled in his line and tied on a larger hook, one with more heft to it. He moved a few steps upriver, threw the braided line across the snagged body, gave it a savage tug, and set the hook deep into her side. He then walked farther down the bank and pulled the corpse free of the willow's branches. The languid current helped him, something his old deadly friend, the Aude, often did.

Please, Saint Peter, let my good luck hold.

Janus was not going to wade out to the body and tow it to shore. The corpse had to come to him. As always, he was mindful of the diviner who had predicted at a Michaelmas fair that cold water, not warm earth, would be his final grave. Fishes, the prey he fed on, would one day take their revenge by feeding on his bloated body.

His watery fate was the fault of his waffling father, who had wavered between the teachings of the Church and the Good Folk for a good three years. Then a Benedictine monk had convinced his father to remain in the Church. So Janus was already speaking when he was baptized.

Everyone knew holy baptism was the rite that saved a man or woman from drowning...but it would not save Janus. The diviner had warned him that though he had been baptized, the ceremony had come too late to protect him. He had already passed the age of infant innocence.

Janus shrugged off worrying about things he couldn't change. Let folks laugh at him: the fisherman who feared water. He was already white-haired and older than most people in privileged Carcassonne and its huddled villages.

Besides, now that he knew how he was going to die, he knew how to delay his death. Janus never waded across the

Aude's shallow places for fear he might be swept away, and he never crossed the river in a boat that might capsize. He never stepped more than waist-deep into any pond or river. Janus intended to live many years yet and continue making his living from the element that would one day kill him.

Once, though, when he was younger and less cautious, he had fallen off a ferry crossing the Aude. Of course, he didn't know how to swim. So instead of clawing for air and floundering and trying foolishly to stand on soft water, he had held his breath and walked along the bottom toward the bank. His head had broken through the surface moments before his desperate lungs ran out of breath.

Now pulling his line in hand-over-hand, he guided the floating corpse into the reeds and eased it closer to the muddy bank. Only then did he take off his woolen cloak and tuck the hem of his tunic into the rope belt around his waist. Mud squished between his knobby toes when he slipped into the cold, thigh-deep water. Wheezing, Janus dragged the dead weight up onto the weedy bank. How could so petite a woman be so heavy?

Fire had blistered her calves and heels. Janus lifted her head with a grunt and slicked tendrils of wet brown hair off her purplish face. He shuddered in surprise. It was Emeline, the woodcutter's daughter.

He glanced in the direction of the charcoalers. Did they have anything to do with this? Had it been an accident?

Janus frowned at a silver chain crossing the back of her neck. He pulled it up until it tightened on her throat. Then he reached underwater and felt a cross hanging on the chain. Emeline was known to hold heretical beliefs. So why was she now wearing a cross?

Janus rubbed his bristling chin with wet fingers. Did he dare take it? His sister could sell it to one of her customers as a relic blessed by some little-known saint. Or he might give it to Cateline. She was to meet him in her cellar this very afternoon while her husband delivered ale to a nearby village.

But to steal a cross might put his immortal soul in danger. He muttered, "Get thee away from my thoughts, Satan."

Why should Emeline die so young? She had been lively as a gnat and pretty as an ivory button. Agbart had three offers of marriage for her. Everybody expected him to accept the fletcher, Sebastian.

Where was her tunic? Had she ripped it off when it caught fire?

Ah well. Janus shrugged. He had no more need to fish today. Even after sharing the finder's fee with Guillaume, he expected good profit from his discovery. To claim his reward, though, he had to catch the *bayle* early at Tisbe's alehouse, then hurry back to guard his trophy.

He hid Emeline's corpse among a patch of reeds close to the shore. Though the current was quiet here, he made certain her body didn't float away by tying her hair around a limb. Then he left her, floating face down with water spiders and minnows dancing around her young body.

As he hurried toward Tisbe's tavern, he rejoiced in his good fortune. Today the alehouse idlers wouldn't taunt him by imitating his stutter or ridiculing his fear of the life-giving river. Instead, to untie his tongue and hear the story of his find, the chandler or the people's lawyer or someone else at the tavern would buy him a mug of ale. He would only hint at the burned chemise and silver cross and not fully tell all of the details until a second mug was set before him.

One thing was certain, Emeline's death meant a second death would follow. The woodcutter had doted on his only surviving daughter. Howling with grief, Agbart would find someone's skull to cleave with his ax.

CHAPTER V

Clanoud had decided to raise the new suckling pig to full growth, but he changed his mind when he saw the gaunt boarling Tolarto's elder son delivered. The stunted, worm-holed cabbages that came with the piglet were only two bites for Lopside, their cart mule. But what had he expected? Tolarto was not one to pay a debt with honor.

Anyway, the runt pig looked likely to die of diarrhea or lung cough or the pox. Tolarto's animals tended to be sickly, thus it was safer to take their profit now.

So within two hours of receiving the little squealer, Bertwoin carried it up to the high-walled *chateau*. After some bargaining, he sold it to the steward for three silver deniers, a high price considering the pig's undernourishment, but the steward knew he could fatten it quickly. The *visconte*, like many noblemen, was fond of a suckling's sweet, tender meat.

Bertwoin then faced the prickly problem of bargaining with his tenacious father over how many coins he must pay for using their mules, equipment, and Wilfraed, his younger brother, when he had plowed Tolarto's squares. Granted, he owed something, but he had done much of the sweat work himself and deserved to earn a good profit from his labor.

His father, as expected, saw the situation as simple: the less his son kept, the more he got.

So Bertwoin sat at the trestle table set up in their *solier*, the house's main room built above the kitchen, and argued with his father over payment.

Clanoud enjoyed fighting with words almost as much as he did with fists. Like many fierce bargainers, he got in the first blow by asking for more than he was likely to receive. He demanded all three deniers and pretended to believe this was a fair rent to pay for the use of his animals and Wilfraed.

Over a mug of slowly sipped ale, Clanoud invented reasons why he should get all the money. He even twisted Bertwoin's generosity to his advantage. Since Bertwoin was willing to give the piglet to Aalis on market day, couldn't he be just as generous with his own family now? If the suckling was of so little worth to him, why did he expect any coins at all?

Finally, Bertwoin laid one silver denier on the table and stood up.

Clanoud said, "This ain't the end of it, boy."

Bertwoin knew his father would never mention it again. If he really thought more than one coin was fair payment, he would never allow any son of his to leave the table.

Bertwoin climbed down the ladder and gave one denier to his *maman* and kept one for himself. An hour later, when in the kitchen with his family, she asked for his remaining coin.

Bertwoin had thought himself openhanded when he gave her a denier and felt her request for the remaining coin as a slap against his generosity. "I earned them. I should have at *least* one for myself."

"You have food and drink and a bed here. What need can you have for it?"

Clanoud sat nearby on a stool while his oldest daughter, Rachel, searched his scalp for lice. He laughed. "So, Ellyn, do you think maybe our son wants to put himself out to stud and buy time with one of Tisbe's alehouse women?"

Bertwoin's younger sister, Maud, stared at him with her mouth open.

Clanoud chuckled. "Or maybe he wants to give the coin to a beggar or leper? Saint Bertwoin is prone to public charity."

"Hah. I was only a kid then."

Not long after twelve-year-old Bertwoin had saved his sister from the boar's attack, while his head still rang with praise, their village priest had delivered a sermon about the Good Samaritan. Bertwoin had promptly gone out, stripped off his tunic, and given it to a leper—a rotting man whose left hand had only three misshapen fingers.

Instead of praising Bertwoin's charity, his *maman* had slapped his ears and scolded him. His father had beaten him and told him he could just walk around in his breeches. Taking pity on him, his *maman* had given him his older sister's extra, hand-me-down tunic to wear. Of course, it fit him like a sausage skin, but it would do until she and her daughters had time to sew him a new tunic.

Now in the kitchen, Ellyn slapped her grown son's chest gently with the back of her hand and shook her head. "You'll be a fool, I guess."

"Then I'll be happy."

"Happy?"

"Who in St. Vincent is more content than the halfwit, Hilario?"

His *maman* laughed. "And it's his family who pays for it.

Don't forget that." Ellyn sat down on a stool and picked up two wool carders. "You're always a quick one with a sly answer, Bertwoin. Just remember, most people won't thank you for it."

"Why do *you* need it?" he asked.

She glanced meaningfully at Rachel's back. The richer his sister's dowry, the more choice they had when picking her husband.

Bertwoin marched outside and fetched the coin from where he had hidden it inside the trunk of an old almond tree.

He handed it to his *maman*. "As you say, I have little need for a silver denier."

His father grinned. "Well now, will you look at that? Our son can be just as generous with his own family as he is with lepers and Aalis."

"Sometimes *maman* is a better bargainer than you are, *Papa*. You took a third of what I had. She took all that I had."

Clanoud slapped his thigh and nodded. "Yes, she'll do that."

His *maman* opened a low chest set against a wall, found the leather pouch she kept inside it for Rachel's dowry, and dropped the clinking coin into it. Rachel watched, her face shining with pride and excitement.

"So now," his *maman* purred, "we have almost enough money to buy you four healthy sheep."

THE *BAYLE* CAME FOR BERTWOIN WHILE HIS FATHER AND Uncle Laurence were in Bram to buy an iron-tipped swing plow from their sister. She was a new widow, and having no sons, had little need for it.

Since farmers were between plowing seasons, Bertwoin

was sleeping late in the warm barn with their brace of idle plow mules and lethargic Lopside. His brother, Wilfraed, slept beside him on clean straw strewn in one corner.

The *bayle* came as quietly as a fox sneaking into a chicken coup, followed by the pig-butcher, Perter Sabatier, who for the price of two tankards of ale had hired on to help the lawman.

It was the pig-man's heavy step on the crisp straw and Lopside shying away from the strangers that woke Bertwoin. He rolled over to find the barrel-bodied *bayle* sneering down at him.

Bertwoin raised his arms to parry a blow. When it didn't come, he realized that though the *bayle* was a man quick to use his staff, he knew it was better not to beat one of Clanoud's sons for no reason.

Bertwoin glared up at the old warrior, blinking in the pale light, his stomach fluttering. Why had the lawman come to menace him?

The *bayle* wore his usual horse-leather tunic with a red crusader's cross on it. A red ribbon held his silk hat in place, its knot mostly hidden in the folds of his meaty chin.

Behind him grinned the lumbering pig-man. Perter, as usual, reeked like a sliced onion, adding his smell to the livestock's stink of sour piss and shit as well as the barn's undertone scent of fresh straw. For a weapon, he carried a wheel spoke made of close-grained oak hard enough to crack a man's bones.

"You'll come," the *bayle* said to Bertwoin, his hand on his knife hilt. He owned a hand-me-down sword, but it was too valuable to bring out for the arrest of a simple plowman. His staff and knife would do.

Wilfraed sat up. "What in the Devil's name are *you* doing here?"

Perter smacked him across the temple with his wheel

spoke. Wilfraed bawled and rolled onto his side, his body trembling in an ague of pain. The pig-man laughed.

Bertwoin jumped up, and both the *bayle* and Perter tensed. But instead of charging the filthy cur, Bertwoin clamped his arms across his chest. A few years before, he would have attacked the grinning pig-butcher and probably been knocked to his knees. He knew now to wait and let rage stoke his revenge. Besides, Wilfraed deserved to have a part in smacking Perter's skull.

For a moment, the *bayle* watched mewling Wilfraed wallow on the stiff straw. "These hind-tit lads nowadays have no bottom to them. Wouldn't have lasted two days with us on the Crusade."

"We'll see how much bottom your pig-butcher has when my father catches him," Bertwoin said.

"Get dressed or we'll take you as you are," the *bayle* growled.

Bertwoin fumbled into his woolen tunic and tied his broad leather belt around his waist, then picked up the pigskin pouch he had used for a rough pillow and shook the ants and fleas off it. To keep Perter from picking through it, he tossed it to where Wilfraed rocked and moaned. He also tossed his knife beside his brother before the *bayle* or Perter took it from him. It was well made, and he didn't want it to get "lost."

The *bayle* nodded toward the barn's door. Instead of wearing his clogs, Bertwoin carried them, clacking, in one hand. If this turned out to be serious business and a chance came for him to run, he wanted to be as barefoot as a rabbit and just as fast.

Why had the *bayle* come for *him*? Had that old skinflint Drouet seen him slip two warm eggs out from under one of his laying hens? He hadn't even needed the eggs. He had stolen them because Drouet had sneered at him and called him a peasant in public. He was one, of course, but it was meant as an insult, and his father would expect him to punish any disrespect, even if it was minor.

"What's this about?" he asked.

The *bayle* didn't answer, and Perter just smiled maliciously and shoved him toward the doorway. They marched outside into a clean August morning still moist from a gentle rain. A pot-bellied sergeant stepped up to make sure Bertwoin waited in place for the pig-man and *bayle* behind him. The sergeant carried only an axe handle and his knife.

His *maman* stood across the bare yard by their cottage, her face ugly with anger.

"Why have you come for him?" she yelled.

"You'll know soon enough, Ellyn," the *bayle* told her.

She spat in his direction. "I know you came sneaking in here while my husband was away."

Bertwoin looked at a fallow field nearby and the woods beyond it and the gray mountains along the horizon. Big as he was, none of these men could catch him once he had five paces on them.

He called out, "You'll need to tend to Wilfraed's head, *Maman*. And tell *papa* it was Perter Sabatier who hit him."

She cried out and ran toward the barn door behind them.

The pig-man lifted his club to strike Bertwoin. The *bayle* stepped between them. "You'll not want to answer to Clanoud for hitting both of his boys, turd-brain." He looked the butcher up and down with disgust. "The squealers you kill have more sense than you do."

"Pigs are smart," Perter said.

Ellyn dodged around them and darted into the barn. The sergeant said, "Trouble," and nodded at something behind the *bayle*.

Perter and the seneschal's lawman turned. Agbart Gasquet and three other woodcutters marched toward them, their manner hostile and determined. The three men carried felling axes. Agbart carried nothing, as if to show that he needed only to rely on his strong, calloused hands.

What did this have to do with them?

The *bayle* looked as solemn as a priest burying a bishop, and the sergeant turned pale. Perter alone seemed at ease. He bit a pine splinter out of his least finger and spat it off the tip of his tongue. Bertwoin figured the pig-man didn't intend to fight woodcutters armed with axes.

Bertwoin saw two magpies picking vermin off their dunghill. Two carrion eaters meant a death was coming, but whose: his, the *bayle's*, Agbart's, or one of his men?

The woodcutters lined up side-by-side and blocked the way out of the yard. Agbart eyed Bertwoin as if he were a viper.

"So is he the one Tolarto saw dancing with my girl?"

"He lied," Bertwoin said. Did the woodcutter really believe he had molested or harmed lovely Emeline?

Agbart kept opening and closing his scarred hands. His eyes were red, probably from crying or a lack of sleep, and his face showed no mercy. Bertwoin stepped two paces backward to put the lawman and more space between him and the woodcutter.

"He's marked for felling," Agbart told the *bayle*, "and I aim to do the chopping. Give him to me and leave in peace. She *was* my daughter." His eyes moistened.

Bertwoin shook his head in disbelief. Agbart had said, "*Was* my daughter." My God, Emeline was dead. This arrest was for a hanging crime, not the mere theft of two chicken eggs.

But who would kill Emeline, the lively cricket who made

everyone smile? And how could anyone believe he had harmed her? He backed farther away from the woodcutters.

"I'll help you find the bastard," Bertwoin cried.

"Stand off, man," the *bayle* growled at Agbart, though it was clear to everyone that the woodcutter was rabid with grief and would obey neither king nor Holy Pope.

The *bayle* stood with his head thrown back, pompous as a young rooster. "Another witness besides Tolarto has stepped forward," he told Agbart. "We'll get a confession from him soon enough. You'll see him hanged and gutted, then drawn and quartered."

Bertwoin flinched. Who was this other witness? Nigellus? What had the interfering little monk accused him of? He had done nothing except flirt a bit with pretty Emeline.

Agbart bellowed and rolled at them like a loose wine barrel.

Bertwoin slid behind Perter.

The woodcutter shoved the startled *bayle* aside before he could use his staff, and the sergeant rushed forward to grapple with Agbart.

When Perter backed two paces away from the fight with his wheel spoke raised, Bertwoin did likewise, but when the pig-butcher stopped, he didn't. He retreated to the barn's doorway.

The *bayle* yelled, "Halt!" at the woodcutters and jabbed one of them in the belly with his staff.

Bertwoin dodged inside the barn and ran through it, not pausing when Wilfraed called out to him. He ducked through a hole in the rear wall and glanced back. His *maman* was shooing the mules toward the main entrance to hinder anyone from chasing him. But the men were still scuffling and cursing.

Bertwoin's muscles felt stiff as cheese from sleep, but he was already running down a rutted path, a clog in either hand, his bare feet slapping damp dirt, when he heard the *bayle* bellow his name.

Bertwoin ran between fields already harvested of grain and turnips, where crows strutted like emperors. He fled uphill toward a forest still swirling with morning mist.

CHAPTER VI.

At dusk, Bertwoin crept out of the pagan woods onto Christian ground. Even little children knew that the rustling night forest was the haunt of grinning imps and demons. He didn't want to hear the menacing sound of cloven hooves clopping behind him.

He stopped in a harvested barley field where three pigs foraged among the stubble under the half-moon. Again he considered his decision. He couldn't go home. The easy choice was to flee to the mountains on the southern horizon and become a shepherd. He and his father had seen Michel, who was probably staying at his uncle's house. Should he toss pebbles against Michel's shutter and go south with him? The *bayle* held no real authority there. In the cool, thin air of the high pastures, rebellious shepherds ruled the landscape.

But even if he fled to the remote mountains, Agbart would come after him like a starving hound chasing a hare. If need be, the ax-wielding woodcutter was willing to hunt him all the way to Hell.

He could claim sanctuary in the brooding Cathedral of Saints Nazarius and Celsus. Agbart, though, might come for him even there. Besides, while imprisoned inside the cathedral, how would he prove himself innocent?

No, his best choice was to run to the alchemist, whose cottage lay on a forest path away from traveled roads and crowded villages. The master alchemist had the ear of *Visconte* Raimon-Rogièr Trencavel and his seneschal, Sir Jean-Luc. They might stop the *bayle* from arresting him until the alchemist trapped the true killer.

The learned master had already used his knowledge, and maybe infidel magic, to solve three murders within the last two years. It was whispered he could worm into a corpse's memory and learn the manner of its death. The alchemist was the one who could find Emeline's murderer, if he was willing to help a fugitive plowman.

When he reached the master's cottage, Bertwoin hid behind a plaited mulberry hedge. What if instead of helping him, the alchemist turned him over to the *bayle*? Somehow, he had to prove to this old man that he hadn't murdered Emeline Gasquet.

As luck would have it, Flowia bustled out of the cottage, carrying an oak bucket. When she stepped through an opening in the hedge, he whispered to her. She whirled and raised the bucket between them.

"It's just me. Bertwoin."

She thumped the bucket down and flicked out her dagger, which she held in front of her breasts. Parts of her glimmered in the moonlight: the silver punched into her leather headband, the silver star at her throat, and even patches of her white apron.

He repeated, "It's Bertwoin."

"I know who you are, plowman," she muttered. "I'm not addled. Everyone's looking under cabbage leaves for you."

If people were searching everywhere for him, he had little chance of not being found. And many of them, judging by

Flowia's distrust, actually believed it possible he had harmed Emeline.

They waited in silence, eying each other, she with her knife pointed at his belly. Na Thea had once described Flowia as a virgin with the heart of a lamb and the bite of a wolf. Her expression didn't look lamblike.

He wasn't sure how to win her favor. She was difficult to predict.

Gossips said Flowia was sassy and overly secure in her position as the alchemist's virgin. They said that without her, the master could not perform his magic and turn base materials into gold. Alchemy required the sun and the moon, male and female, old and young.

Bertwoin's stomach gurgled from hunger. Flowia laughed and seemed less afraid of him now, as if his stomach had argued against his guilt.

"It is said you once knew hunger too," he snapped.

She was born, fatherless, at an inn near the Saint-Hilaire Abbey. Her mother, mad they said with religious remorse, died soon after birthing her.

The innkeeper's wife had kept the orphaned brat, raised her, and used her as a servant until she was old enough to sell to a traveling troupe of actors. When Flowia ran away from the troupe, she came begging to the alchemist's door for bread and beer...a piteous sight: thin as a stick, lethargic from hunger, almost fainting, her bare feet bleeding from stone cuts.

Like a stray dog once fed, Flowia continued to skulk around the master's cottage. When the traveling troupe found her by accident, the master bought her from them. The gossips said he'd never regretted his purchase.

"Hunger, yes," she said, "but no one pursued me for murder."

"I know now how the hunted boar feels. Only the brainless would chase me for such a crime."

"A witness named you." Though she had lowered her knife, she kept it between them. "The *bayle* means to catch you and see the *chatelain* torture a confession out of you."

"But how can anyone believe *I* would harm little Emeline?"

She raised the knife, its point still aimed at his belly. "How do you know you are accused of killing Emeline?"

So she had set a trap for him by not telling him who the victim was. Bertwoin realized his face was tight as leather stretched across a drum, so he took a slow breath and loosened his jaw. "Agbart came for me. When he and the *bayle* scuffled, I ran. And I remember you telling my father and me at the Devil's Doorstep that he was searching for Emeline. So where did they find her body?"

Flowia pointed her knife at a tiny spring spurting from between two rocks. "I am in need of water."

"And I need the master's help."

"He already has enough demands on his time," she growled. She studied at his face in the dim moonlight and must have recognized he was desperate. "Then you had better fetch water for me, hadn't you?"

Bertwoin grumbled, "I'm a stag caught between the dogs and the huntsman."

He picked up the oak bucket and shuffled to the bubbling gush of water while Flowia waited near the opening in the hedge. His father would snarl to see him treated like a servant by the alchemist's virgin and would beat him for letting her shame him and their family in this way.

The spring's fresh smell made him realize his throat was dry as chalk, so before doing this chore for Flowia, he drank cold water from his cupped hand and slaked his thirst. Then he filled the wooden bucket, lugged it to her, and set it at her bare feet.

"Did your master create this spring?" he asked.

"I don't know. It was here when I came, and I'm elated to have it. I don't have to walk halfway to town to visit a dangerous well."

He nodded. Most wells were nothing more than communal holes in the ground. It wasn't uncommon for women and young girls to slip in the slick mud surrounding these holes, fall in, and drown. "I'm surprised the master doesn't just have the buckets fill themselves."

She pointed her knife at him. "You have an ungrateful manner, plowman. You mock the master you've come to beg for help."

"It wasn't mockery."

When Flowia glanced down at the water in her bucket, moonlight glinted off the silver decorating her headband. "Janus the fisherman has related the story of his finding Emeline at least twenty times by now. Everyone knows it."

"Everyone except the one the *bayle* came to arrest." He jabbed his broad chest with his thumb. "The one who hid among the trees and talked to no one except squirrels and birds."

She nodded. "I smell the green forest on you. So even using hounds, they couldn't locate you."

"I'm not Janus. My odor is not so strong that maggots take me for a corpse. And I don't fear water." He saw she understood that he had walked in streams to hide his scent.

He listened intently as she told Janus's tale of finding Emeline. When she finished, he stared a moment at the water reflecting the half-moon in her oak bucket. "What fiend would wish to harm her?"

Flowia was hunched forward in a posture of sorrow. "She hoped to be married before the next harvest."

He slapped his thigh in anger. "Charcoalers worked nearby. And Tolarto was roaming the woods. He lied when he told Agbart I danced with Emeline. They need to investigate them."

"Brother Nigellus saw *you* with Emeline on the day she disappeared, or so he states."

So he had been right in guessing that Brother Nigellus was the second witness mentioned by the *bayle*. "That meddlesome monk? He lied too if he said I danced with her."

Flowia put a hand on her hip. "What *were* you doing with her?"

"What? We crossed paths. There's nothing in that. We've known each other all our lives." Bertwoin held up a hand, palm forward. "I didn't do her any harm. I will swear so on the Bible."

Flowia looked unimpressed at his willingness to take an oath of innocence. "Brother Nigellus told the *bayle* that you and she greeted each other in the manner of heretics, then the two of you danced lewdly together on the riverbank."

Bertwoin stared at Flowia with his mouth open. Nigellus had turned out to be far more vicious than meddlesome. "That mean, lying sack of pig shit. Why is he trying to kill me?"

Was the little monk jealous of their laughing and flirting together?

Flowia murmured, "If he is lying, we must find out why." She fingered the star hanging at her throat. "We must also learn why the bottom of Emeline's chemise was burned, and why Janus found her wearing a cross."

"A cross? I don't remember her wearing one when we met."

Flowia whispered, "Well, it is poor Agbart who bears the cross now."

Bertwoin sighed. After Agbart's wife and two of his children had died, Emeline had been the only woman left in his house. Now she too was gone. Only a son, an apprentice to a chandler, was left to care for him in his old age.

Flowia sucked in her lips and told him, "After you scampered off into the woods, Agbart visited the master. He came as barefoot as a pilgrim and clinked four silver deniers on the table. 'That's everything I've got at this time,' he said, 'but I'll supply you with wood this winter as payment. Find the plowman for me. I want him, even if it costs my very soul.'"

Bertwoin reared back. "He'd bargain away his holy soul?"

"Agbart is beyond fear or reason. He wept like Job did over the loss of his ten children. You know how bottomless his pride was for Emeline. 'She just walked out to pick blackberries and rue and mushrooms,' he said over and over again."

"Can the master find the killer?"

Flowia blew out a breath. "Your question does you no credit, plowman. When I first came to him, and he paid two gold coins for me, far more than I was worth, I doubted him. What I didn't know then was that the gold would flake off in the actors' hands a day or so down the road and leave them holding lead." She smiled at their punishment. "He despises those who buy and sell people."

Bertwoin almost blurted out that the master must then despise himself, because he had bought and paid for her. As his *maman* had warned, he was often too quick with his ready replies. But he had caught himself in time. This was different. The master had rescued Flowia from slavery and abuse.

She looked Bertwoin directly in the eye, as a pig will do. "In four years of serving him, I've learned not to doubt what he can do."

She scanned their surroundings. A breeze purred through a nearby orchard, spreading the scent of ripe apples across the night and making the weeds in a nearby field seem to whisper secrets.

"Come," she said, "the master will want to speak with you as much as you want to speak with him."

She slipped her knife into its leather scabbard and looked meaningfully at the bucket on the ground. He laughed and picked it up. She turned and glided through the opening in the mulberry hedge that led to the cottage door.

As he followed her like a noblewoman's servant, Bertwoin said to her retreating back, "Two gold coins, even real ones, would have been a bargain for you."

She spun around, her mouth open, and studied his face to see if he was laughing at her. Then she nodded to thank him for the compliment.

Now all he had to do was convince the master to rescue him.

CHAPTER VII

The mulberry hedge enclosed a poultry yard, and an alert goose honked to protest Bertwoin's intrusion into its space. The others gathered into a hissing group. Ignoring them, Flowia glided to the house, which, like the alchemist's separate workshop, had the usual wattle-and-daub walls and shingle roof.

Bertwoin carried the sloshing bucket to the front door and paused. It wasn't a witch's den, but still, people whispered about the alchemist. What price would he demand for the use of his pagan magic?

Bertwoin stepped inside a wide front room with a bench and an oak chest shoved against a wall. A colorful tapestry hung over the furniture, its scene showing men hunting a unicorn.

Green rushes covered the dirt floor. The room was clean, candle-lit, and smelled of boiled beans, roast pork, and something else, something flowery and cathedral-like.

Beyond the front room lay the kitchen, "the house within a house," built of stone instead of wattle-and-daub to protect it from fire.

The master, who was white-haired and weathered, sat on a three-legged milking stool in the large kitchen, cutting slices off a green apple with a Moorish dagger. He was thin and long as a strop and wore an ankle-length red robe and sandals. Like Bertwoin's father and the *bayle*, he had traveled with King Philip II to the Holy Land in 1190, though the monks at the local abbey claimed he had spent as much time during the Crusade with the infidels as he had with his Christian brothers.

Bertwoin remembered his father once telling him, "Men like the alchemist and *bayle* may go off to the Holy Land, but that doesn't mean they come back one whit holier."

Then again, marching off to the Holy Land hadn't turned his father into a saint either. Instead, it had bedeviled him with battle memories and dreams that sometimes caused him to sleepwalk at night. He would cry out to dead people and beg forgiveness. Did the alchemist also have these nightmares?

The master didn't seem surprised to see a young plowman wanted for murder carry water into his home. Had he fore-known Bertwoin was coming?

"He admits," Flowia told the alchemist, "that he met poor Emeline just before she was murdered. But he denies that he and Emeline performed the Good Folk greeting or that they danced together."

"Indeed," the master mumbled. "So why did both Tolarto and the monk lie? Well, young man, tell me about meeting her that day."

Flowia pointed to a bench beside a kitchen table stacked with clean dishes. Bertwoin dodged a ham and a plucked hen hanging from a smoke-blackened roof beam and sat down.

A ladder led to an upper chamber, a *solier*, usually the most comfortable room in a house. Bertwoin frowned at a faint haze that drifted like a ghost out of its doorway.

Watching him, the master chuckled. "We enjoy the smell of incense, as do those who attend mass."

Did they use it to perform pagan ceremonies?

Opposite the bedrooms was a small door in the kitchen's wall. Bertwoin assumed it led into a cellar, where barrels were kept and maybe beds for visitors. This door and the main one in front were the only two exits if he needed to escape.

Bertwoin measured the house with his shrewd peasant's eye, noting the luxury of its space and the privacy it offered. Few prosperous merchants in Carcassonne or the suburbs down-slope from the citadel lived better than this master alchemist and his virgin.

Flowia bustled about, setting out a feast of goat's cheese, cold chicken, wheat bread, and warm red ale on the table. Her movements were almost a dance. Bertwoin eyed the repast with delight. Yes, the master and Flowia did live and eat well.

As Bertwoin told of his meeting with Emeline, he watched the alchemist's face for disbelief and saw none. He ended by offering to plow six squares if the master would prove him blameless.

The old man's weathered face crinkled with mirth. "And to think, Agbart was here this very morning, asking me to conjure you out of your hole. You made it an easy trick, boy." He pointed to the food Flowia had set out on the table. "Eat. The belly is a selfish organ that thinks only of its own comfort."

"Sounds like a bishop," Bertwoin quipped and cringed inwardly. His joke sounded common, like something a witless peasant would say.

The master considered him a moment, then his smile faded. "Emeline Gasquet is another matter. We'll use logic and guile to conjure up her slayer. Though luck is always a welcome visitor. We'll need it."

Bertwoin ducked his head to thank the alchemist for believing he was innocent. The master tossed the apple core he held into a bucket and sheathed his ornate dagger.

"Why does the *bayle* not suspect the charcoalers?" Bertwoin asked. "They use fire day and night, and Flowia said Emeline's chemise was burned."

"He has two witnesses against you," the old man said.

"Tolarto I understand," Bertwoin said. "He's my enemy, but I have no idea why Brother Nigellus wants me dead."

The master slapped the kitchen table. "I wish I could examine her corpse before they clean it for burial."

Flowia dipped water from the bucket Bertwoin had carried in and poured it into a copper pan. "I have heard," she said, "that nuns will come to the abbey tomorrow to wash the body for burial."

"How do they know for certain anyone murdered her?" Bertwoin asked. "Could she not have drowned?"

Flowia shook her head. "Because of the violence done to her. They know she didn't kill herself, and so, she may lie in holy ground. The mortal sin lies not with her but with her attacker."

"So she had changed back to the faith of the Church?"

Wary now, Flowia turned to face him. "I do not believe so."

"But she wore a cross. And you say she will lie in hallowed ground. Would the Church allow a heretic to lie in its graveyard?"

Flowia squared her body toward him. "You think she should not lie in sanctified ground?"

"You thrust thoughts in my head that aren't there. I think Emeline has less sin on *her* soul than Bishop Othon does on his."

Flowia relaxed her aggressive stance. "The bishop likes to live warm in winter. He knows Agbart and the other woodcutters are necessary for him to do so." She shrugged. "So the bishop pretends she repented."

"It is strange, though," she continued, "that Emeline wore a silver cross. She would rather wear a leper's cloak. But if the bishop and abbot find it convenient to believe she had returned to their faith, why argue with them? Burial in consecrated ground will ease Agbart's fear for his daughter's soul."

The master rubbed two of his fingers against his thumb. "Agbart, it is said, also promised a sizable donation to the abbey."

"But why should he care?" Bertwoin asked. "The churchyard is no more sacred to Agbart than a field of barley."

The alchemist leaned forward with his elbows on his knees. "The woodcutter holds the bread of the Church in one hand and the Good Folks' sacred book in the other. Emeline died before a Good Man or Woman could give her the final sacrament. So, her soul is doomed to return for another life in another body. The Church and its prayers offer her salvation when the Good Folks offer her only a second life in our world of evil and woe."

Bertwoin frowned. "Wouldn't she have to come back anyway? Good Man Hugues preaches that not even a Good Woman like Gertrude can reach final rest. Only a man's soul can join the good god in heaven."

The master looked at Bertwoin with pity. Flowia snatched the goat's cheese and wheat bread away from him.

"And you believe this?" she snapped.

He held up his hands, one of them still holding a piece of bread she hadn't taken. "I'm only saying this is what Good Man Hugues preaches."

She put the cheese and bread on a small side table, came back, and took away his ale. He looked at the master for help, but the old man watched them with amused curiosity and said nothing.

Flowia muttered, "Do you also believe Good Men and Good Women kiss the pink asses of tomcats? That they sacrifice babies and eat their ashes?"

Bertwoin held his tongue. If he angered her more than he already had, she might put a curse on him or tell the *bayle* he had visited the master.

Flowia waited for his answer with her arms crossed under her breasts. He touched his forehead with his fingers and flipped them to show he had no thoughts on the subject.

"So," the master said, ending the argument.

Bertwoin could have kissed the alchemist's bony hand.

The master sat up straight on his three-legged stool. "So the monks have carried her body to the abbey. They will take better care of her now than they ever did while she was alive."

Bertwoin grunted in agreement. But would Emeline have wanted to be buried in the churchyard? She had sympathized with the Good Folk, and like them, she had wanted to live a simple, blameless life. The Good Folk provided service to others and endured hardship as the Apostles had done. They were of the people, unlike Bishop Othon, who wore cloaks woven of silk and gold thread, or Abbot Jehan, who was more concerned with what was served at his table than how he served the community.

Bertwoin looked wistfully at his mug of ale on the side table. It was time for him to be of service. "I can get you into the abbey unseen, master."

"Even monks lock their gates."

"Not all of them. A back door in the abbey's church is left unlocked. Business sometimes keeps monks out late at night. With luck, we can sneak into the abbey when the brothers are not at their prayers. I know the way to the chamber where the dead are prepared."

The alchemist chuckled. "Plowman, if you studied religion with the same zeal you study the abbey's doings, you might become an abbot."

Bertwoin pretended to be shocked. "God forbid. Then my flabby soul would be doomed."

The master studied him with a glint of mischief in his dark eyes. "So how is it that a plowman knows of this unlocked door?"

"I've helped some brothers do business with farmers and merchants."

"And this business must be done in secret after dark?"

"The abbot forbids many things to his monks that he doesn't forbid to himself."

Flowia put her fists on her hips and glared at Bertwoin. "Do you bring them women?"

He reared back, offended, and turned to the master, his hands up in entreaty. "Why do women always think the worst of us?"

The alchemist smiled. "Because they know us, young man, they know us." He shook his head in mock despair. "And they are often right."

Bertwoin told Flowia, "No, I do not sneak women in for the monks' pleasure. We bring them pork when they aren't allowed meat, gambling dice, messages, and warm furs in winter. On my last visit, we brought healing seeds to Brother Theodoric."

He started to defend his honor further, but the master raised a skeletal hand to stop him. "If caught there, it might be your death. And it will be the dungeon for me. The abbot would relish the chance to tweak the nose of our young *visconte*, my protector. A charge of desecration against me would seem a gift from God to him."

The hatred of Abbot Jehan for *Visconte* Raimon-Rogièr was well known.

It was said that Satan had taught the alchemist thirteen

magical skills while he was in the Holy Land. One of these was how to turn base metals into gold. *Visconte* Raimon-Rogièr was said to take a share of all this new gold. Not wanting to lose such an easy source of wealth, the *visconte* had more than once publicly protected the alchemist.

"I do not make gold, plowman. I only fashion what the *visconte's* seneschal gives me. Like all men, I am bound by God's natural laws." He held up a forefinger. "I am, though, an alchemist too. I conduct experiments to learn nature's laws. Matter mirrors the spirit. I seek to learn the secrets that will purify my soul. True alchemy is not really about making gold. It is about changing ignorance into wisdom. Spirit must be brought down into this world of sight and touch and made manifest." The master chuckled. "And so ends my sermon."

"Amen," Bertwoin quipped. He took a deep breath, then put his precious life at risk. "If it will help you find Emeline's killer, I will slip you into the abbey like a fox entering a chicken coop."

"Though you risk torture and a hanging?"

"Even so, master."

He nodded at Bertwoin. "The *bayle* and *chatelaine* are experts at extracting confessions. But they are none too exact about the true guilt of those they torture." The master scratched his bearded chin. "The woodcutter deserves to know who stole away the daughter he cherished above all treasure."

"So you do believe me? You think I am innocent."

"Flowia does, or you wouldn't be sitting at my table. She rarely errs in judging character." The master rose stiffly from the stool. "Do not misunderstand me, Bertwoin. I think she spies faults in your character, but murder is not one of them."

The alchemist smiled at her. "Bring both my blue and brown cloaks, daughter. They'll help disguise us. I'll also want my belt and pouch."

Flowia glided into one of the bedrooms.

The master nodded at the ladder leading up to the *solier*. "You can rest up there. I will work in my laboratory until the early hours of the morning and wake you then. The monks must be sound asleep when we sneak into their abbey."

Bertwoin doubted he would get any sleep.

CHAPTER VIII.

They left after matins, three hours before dawn. The woolen cowl of the master's brown cloak that Bertwoin wore drawn over his head smelled faintly of sulfur. Would the devilish chemical make his hair fall out?

He smiled as he led the master through a dark orchard of sweet-scented pear trees. Both the dour, red-nosed Abbot Jehan and thorny Sir Jean-Luc—on behalf of *Visconte* Raimon-Rogièr— claimed this orchard as their property. Last autumn, the seneschal had let the abbot steal, as he called it, the rent from this orchard. Then he had insulted the cleric by sending soldiers to the unprotected abbey to seize the payment. Abbot Jehan, of course, was indignant and protested this sacrilege. He had also claimed that the soldiers had pillaged his treasury and taken far more than just the single payment given to him for rental of the pear orchard.

So, yes, the master was right in saying the abbot would delight in catching the *visconte's* alchemist inside his abbey.

Wanting to make certain they weren't seen, Bertwoin decided to avoid using the main wooden bridge over the brooding Aude. Instead, he decided to ferry the master across the dark river in a canvas shell with a wickerwork frame. During the day, pilgrims and beggars used this tiny boat to row across to the abbey, the pilgrims coming to worship Saint Nazarius's shinbone, the beggars coming for brown bread and weak beer.

The alchemist hesitated. "You propose to cross our local version of the River Styx at night in a shell? Have you done this before?"

"Yes, master." Bertwoin had no idea where the River Styx lay. Had the master stood on its bank in the Holy Land or read of it in one of his parchments? "Is this River Styx dangerous?"

"Aren't all rivers treacherous, especially at night? Does not our Aude drown even those who can swim?"

But the alchemist climbed into the boat and sat quietly with his hood up while Bertwoin rowed him to the other bank without mishap.

So with only God's stars, the half-moon, and a few stray clouds to witnesses their trespass, Bertwoin led the way to the unlocked door set in the massive back wall of the abbey's church. He eased it open. A single candle at the front door glowed in the solemn stillness. He slipped inside into chilly darkness, hoping no praying monk lay prostrate on the stone floor. The master pulled his cloak tighter and joined him.

Bertwoin closed the back door and listened for the murmur of a brother's prayer or the scuff of a sandal in some dark corner. Were it not consecrated, the church might seem a fitting haunt for wraiths and demons. It had the same menacing hush as the Devil's Doorstep. The moon's milky glow threw distorted and elongated colors from the shapes in the stained-glass windows across aisles and benches. Bertwoin reminded himself that this church was not menacing. Only his fear of being caught made it seem so. It was holy. He inhaled deeply to savor the faint scent of frankincense that lingered in the cool air.

Bertwoin and the alchemist glided like ghosts down a side aisle to the main doors. Bertwoin dipped two fingers into the font and made the sign of the cross. He then creaked one of the front doors open and peeked outside at the rectangular courtyard enclosed by the abbey's imposing inner buildings. For two breaths, he stared with longing at the waist-high stone wall circling the well in the center. Fear had parched his mouth, but he dared not draw water from it now to slake his thirst.

No black-robed monks were in sight. Bertwoin glanced back at the silent alchemist to see if he was ready, then darted to the sheltered gallery running along the courtyard's left side. He hurried down the covered walkway, passing open rooms until he came to the chamber for the dead. It stank like a privy.

"You have luck," he whispered to the alchemist. "They've not yet washed her body for burial. The nuns are probably coming from Bram."

The master seemed more resigned than pleased. "I believe our noses will not call it luck. Ah well, now we know for certain her body floated face down. The river didn't wash her backside clean."

Once inside the reeking cell, the master told Bertwoin, "Stand guard at the entrance." The cell was so small, Bertwoin could lean in and touch the granite altar from the doorway.

Wasting no time, the alchemist lit a tallow candle spiked on an iron cross and moved it to the waist-high granite slab in the center of the room where Emeline lay on her back. Bertwoin's throat constricted. She had been a songbird with a heart-lifting voice that would never be heard again.

He swallowed to relieve the lump of anger stuck in his

throat. Her eyes stared sightlessly at the low ceiling. Her face was pulpy, waterlogged. He clenched his hands into fists and wished he could catch the killer before anyone else did. The murderer had slashed her cheeks and slit open her nostrils. Why? To mar her beauty? To torture her? Had she been alive when he did this?

The master peered into her gaping mouth full of shadow and blew out his breath. "Her tongue has been sliced in half. Probably while she was alive. How did the killer to do this without getting his fingers bitten?"

Someone else, probably a monk, had dabbed a crude red cross on her forehead to protect her corpse from roving demons. Bertwoin muttered, "Instead of worrying about devils now, they should have protected her from a human demon while she was still alive."

The alchemist glanced at him, his expression grim. "That was beyond anyone's doing. Even her formidable father couldn't protect her."

The master lifted her head and examined it. "No scalp wound. She has been dead at least two or three days." He examined her throat. "As I thought. He choked her into submission instead of knocking her senseless."

He folded the top of the sacking under her swollen chin back over her breasts. She wore only a filthy white undergarment, another sign no one had yet tended to the body. After washing little Emeline with blessed water and rubbing her corpse with scented oil, the nuns would wrap it in white linen for the final funeral rites and burial.

"Why bother to cover her corpse with sacking?" Bertwoin muttered. "She cannot feel the cold now."

The master hummed disagreement. "Dignity is never out of place. It was done for the living, not the dead."

Bertwoin watched the alchemist while continually glancing outside for monks. The master pulled the hemp covering farther back, raising a sluggish moth that flittered to a rough wall and clung there. The alchemist then folded the sacking over her knees and lower legs. Bertwoin turned back to the courtyard, more to take a breath of clean night air than to watch for wandering monks. The old man had a strong stomach. The stink was thick enough to put a layer of scum on their woolen cloaks.

When Bertwoin glanced back into the cell, he saw that the alchemist had set aside the hemp cloth and had pulled Emeline's linen chemise, its bottom hem burned, up to her neck. Her delicate feet and brown shins were blistered.

Emeline's slender body shone in the candlelight, naked, her skin gray. The inside of her left breast showed a gash washed bloodless by the Aude, and her ribs were scoured with scratches. A silver cross on a chain lay between her breasts.

"Odd," murmured Bertwoin. When the master looked up, he added, "The abbey sells these crosses for corpses, but Janus says he found her body already wearing one. Flowia thinks she stayed unrepentant. So if she didn't believe the rood should be honored, why wear one?"

The grizzled alchemist grunted. "Our question, then, is what murderer is rich enough to give the dead a silver cross? And why do so? Mockery? Regret?"

The master pointed to her wrists marked with a thick, repeated pattern. "Hands tied with a braided rope. That rules out repentant self-mutilation and suicide."

Bertwoin whispered a prayer for Emeline's wandering soul. After such a horrendous death, it was possible, and maybe even likely, that her restless ghost would haunt the place where it had been ripped from its body.

As if he had heard Bertwoin's thoughts, the master frowned. "We must find where this killer lit his fire and tortured her. If she died after dark, as I believe she did, why did no one, a night fisherman or passing pilgrim or townsman or someone staggering home late from a tavern, see the blaze?"

The master bent closer to Emeline. "There's a wound in her side, a small hole, but I believe the cause was Janus's fish-hook." He inspected her whitish-gray hands with care. "She fought her murderer. Two of her fingernails are ragged. Though she could have broken them earlier doing some mundane chore."

The alchemist pulled a scrap of linen out of the pouch hanging from his ox-hide belt, drew his Moorish dagger, and scraped debris from under her fingernails onto the cloth. Folding the linen, he tucked it into his leather pouch.

He examined her private parts. Bertwoin hummed in disapproval. Did this not violate Emeline's dignity?

"She was not defiled." The alchemist glanced around the tiny cell. "If anything else was found with her, where would it be now?"

"Maybe in the beggars' room," Bertwoin suggested. "The abbey stores its charity there for the poor. It's near the kitchen and gathering hall."

"Ah well, we'll not risk it then. We must accept what Flowia heard, that Janus found her wearing only this chemise and the rood."

The faraway sound of a cough startled Bertwoin. He stepped back to the doorway and peeked down the corridor. A candle's light brightened the far end of the gallery. He hissed a warning.

The master licked his thumb and index finger, pinched out their candle's white flame, and covered Emeline's body again with the hemp sacking. He then wrapped his blue cloak around himself, backed into a dark corner nearest the doorway, and seemed to disappear. A monk would have to come into the chamber to see him.

Bertwoin darted around the altar and squatted behind it.

The edges of its sturdy granite base were carved into an ornate latticework. He peered through a diamond-shaped opening at the doorway and listened to sandals slap the gallery's walkway. It wasn't a single brother. *Sancta Maria, please don't let monks come to pray over Emeline's body now.*

Bertwoin adjusted his cloak's cowl as if that would hide him better. His heart bounced under his ribcage. His hands turned as cold as an iron hinge on a snowy Christmas Day.

A monk carrying a lit candle marched past the room's doorway. His face forward, his expression resolute, he ignored their dark chamber. Bertwoin let out his breath. Another passed their cell, followed by another as a line of silent, black-robed brothers shuffled by on their way toward the church.

Were they going to pray? Why now? It was too early for lauds.

Then a monk stopped at the doorway. Bertwoin sucked in a breath. He didn't dare move, not even to duck away from his eyehole. It was little, righteous Nigellus, his accuser. Did he regret not saving Emeline's soul or think she had gotten what she deserved? Nigellus murmured a quick prayer, made the sign of the cross, then moved on.

Before Bertwoin could relax, blond Brother Gregorius stepped into view and also stopped. He resembled a skeleton covered with sallow skin. One hand was bandaged, and Bertwoin remembered his sister saying this fanatical monk had held his hand in a candle's flame to test his faith. Bertwoin almost snorted in contempt. Lashing his back bloody wasn't enough self-torture for this zealot. All must see his mortification and witness his devotion to God. All must know that he was the most pious of all the abbey brothers.

Why did this damned Breton monk stare into their chamber? Did he sense that they hid inside it?

Instinctively, Bertwoin reached under his woolen cloak for the hilt of his knife, then remembered he had left it with

Wilfraed in their barn. It didn't matter. He would try to fight his way through the monks, but he would never kill one of them. Besides, stabbing Brother Gregorius would turn the monk into a martyred saint.

A gaunt hand appeared behind Brother Gregorius and pushed him forward as gently as a mother directing her balky child. Stern Prior Simon then stepped into the doorway and raised his smoking candle. His eyes glittered like fish scales in the white light. He looked with sorrow at hemp-covered Emeline. Then he made the sign of the cross with his free hand and walked on.

Sighing, Bertwoin collapsed backward and sat on the cell's cold, stone floor.

The alchemist stepped out of his dark corner. "Now, I think, is a good time for us to leave."

"But the brothers are in the church."

"The abbey has many doors," the master reminded him.

Bertwoin grimaced at his own stupidity. "Fear has addled my brain. Of course, there are many doors, all with their bolts on the *inside*. But we won't be able to relock it."

"Ah well, some brother neglected his duty tonight."

Bertwoin agreed with a nod. "Or whoever finds it unlocked might believe another monk went out earlier than he did."

After stepping outside of the stinking chamber, Bertwoin saw stray clouds had massed into a dark fleece that now veiled the half-moon. Had they been in the room so long? The air smelled fresh and drizzle formed a film on their cloaks.

The master began to lead Bertwoin down the covered gallery toward the abbey's front wall where two huge oak doors reinforced with black iron guarded the main entrance. Beside these formal doors was a small one for monks to use for their everyday business.

They were only halfway down the gallery when someone on the other side of the courtyard yelled at them. The master flitted behind a pillar. Bertwoin did the same and peeked around it.

An indignant brother marched toward them. When he reached the well in the courtyard's center, he yelled again. Bertwoin cursed him. It was just their luck for a monk to be late to prayers and see them. And wasn't it good fortune for this tardy monk? In the excitement of discovering an intruder, Prior Simon might forget to punish the brother's lateness.

Bertwoin realized he must save the master, so he turned and ran back down the gallery toward the church, away from the front wall. He darted into an archway on his right and dashed through a short, covered walkway, then sprinted into the grounds between the abbey's inner buildings and its high outer wall.

Bertwoin hadn't run five paces toward the main doors at the abbey's front when he glanced back and saw the brother burst around the corner behind him. The monk had to be God-possessed to run so fast.

Bertwoin raced along the building. His goal was an archway that led back to the courtyard and the abbey's front entrance. He prayed the master had left the small door open for him.

Ten paces before the archway, he was yanked backwards. The brother had grabbed the back of his cloak. He moaned. How could any monk be so fast? Bertwoin dodged left, but the hand held tight and slowed his run to a struggling walk.

So let the monk catch a wolf instead of a rabbit. Bertwoin twisted and jerked the surprised monk toward him. He put the brother in a headlock and punched his nose. The monk bawled like an injured calf and let go of Bertwoin's cloak.

Leaving the young monk lying on the grass, Bertwoin ran

to the archway and dashed through it. Mist whipped his face when he stepped into the open courtyard.

He trotted to the small door. Two monks stood in front of the church at the other end of the courtyard, scanning the misty enclosure to see why someone had yelled.

One of them pointed at Bertwoin and shouted, "There he is. A trespasser. Stop!"

Bertwoin recognized Prior Simon's voice. He jerked open the unlocked small door, jumped outside, and slammed it shut. He fled down the abbey's front wall and disappeared around a corner. At least now they would have to guess which way the rabbit had run.

He raced toward the river, hoping the alchemist was already there. But when he reached the canvas shell on the bank, it was empty. Where had the master gone? He shoved the boat into the dark water and looked around. Had the alchemist decided to use the bridge? Far behind him, Bertwoin heard monks yelling.

A nearby rustling sound made him turn. A figure stepped out from behind a tree and came toward him. Bertwoin recognized the master and grunted, grateful that the alchemist had waited to see if he had escaped before using the boat to save himself.

The old man climbed into the wobbly shell held against the bank for him. Bertwoin then pushed it away and jumped into it. As he rowed them out into the Aude, he let the shell drift downstream to put more distance between them and the pursuing monks. The voices behind them grew fainter. Mist drifted over the brooding water.

The master whispered, "I thank you, plowman, for taking all of the pursuit onto yourself. Not only was it kind to save me, but it was also the smart thing to do. I run like a crippled beggar and would certainly have been caught."

Bertwoin glanced up at the faintly lit spot in the clouds

where the half-moon hid. The monks were now too far away to hear or see them.

The alchemist sat in the bobbing shell as if he were a king traveling down the river in a royal barge. "Were you recognized?"

"Maybe." Bertwoin shrugged as if it were of no concern. "Probably. But I don't think the brother saw who you were."

"That bodes well for me, but I fear our outing dropped you deeper into mishap."

"Did you find the clues you needed, master?"

"I learned much from examining her corpse."

"Then going to the abbey was worth the trouble."

"What did you think of the monks we saw?" the master asked.

"Not much. Most of them ignored the chamber. Brother Nigellus did acknowledge Emeline's corpse, Brother Gregorius seemed almost to sense us, and Prior Simon seemed to grieve her death."

"Did you not mark guilt on the prior's face?"

"Guilt?" Bertwoin remembered the glittering eyes. "No, I saw sorrow. We all know he tolerates the Good Folk much more than the abbot does. I've heard he was gentle with Emeline."

Bertwoin huffed in anger. "Agbart may have spoiled Emeline like a royal princess, but she always did her duty. And she was as chipper as a sparrow, always singing and hopping about. She was full of promise." He slapped his oar on the river's broad back. "What slavering cur would torture her? And why? There could be no profit in killing her."

"The murderer had the demon of lead in him."

"Lead carries a demon in it? Is that why you drink from a copper goblet?"

"You'll sleep in my cellar," the alchemist said, ignoring his questions. "Try not to ruffle Flowia's patience too much."

"You are generous to risk hiding me."

The alchemist's lips twisted into a playful smile. "Have you not agreed to plow for me? I will hold you to that bargain."

"You risk your livelihood for my plowing?"

Chuckling, the master said, "Perhaps, young Bertwoin, you are right." He leaned sideways, dipped his long fingers into the cold river, and flicked away the drops. "If you are caught, I will wash my hands of you as Pontius Pilate did with Jesus. I will claim you sneaked into my cellar without my knowing it."

They bumped against the bank on the other side. Bertwoin held the canvas shell still so the thin, old man could clamber out, then pulled the boat up into the weeds.

As they began walking side-by-side along the bank, the master asked, "You think I am a fool to store you in my cellar?"

Bertwoin agreed with a shrug. "I thank you for it. But who would ever believe an alchemist didn't know when a murderer slept in his house?"

The master hummed, accepting his argument. "True, but you did save me just now from the monks in the abbey. And you will not abide in my house long. In ten days, a carter takes supplies to the mountains. He will show you where our shepherds pasture our sheep."

The master glanced eastward where the drizzle had become lighter. "Come, we must now find the place where the murderer tortured Emeline and see what story it has to tell us. A fire at night would be seen. And how did Emeline end up in the river? Fire and water. Together they hint at something."

"And you wish me to go with you now?"

"Yes. We just have time to get there before the cock crows. No one will spy us once we are in the forest."

Bertwoin looked back in the direction of the abbey. "Well, the brothers probably won't cross the river."

The master patted his shoulder. "Don't fret. I have solved mysteries for Sir Jean-Luc and his lawmen in the past. And the seneschal will want me to find this murderer before he kills again."

"You think it possible?"

"Possible? More than that, I think it likely."

CHAPTER IX.

As the master had predicted, no one saw them scurry over the wooden bridge. And as they walked along the river path behind the grain mill, Bertwoin warned, "It's good fishing weather for Janus."

The old man flapped a hand as if flicking away a fly. "Janus doesn't need rain to enhance his luck. He has skill and could catch an eel in a desert." He smiled. "Would he get a fee for catching you? But then, hooking a big fish is not the same as landing it, is it? A monk found that out this morning." The master seemed pleased by the idea of Janus trying to capture Bertwoin. "Still, it might be rather awkward for both of us if he did see you, but we have to find the place where Emeline was tortured. Rain will wash the earth clean and wipe away the story it has to tell us. Let us hope this hasn't already happened."

The master brushed a film of mist off the shoulders of his cloak. "Moreover, Janus might not recognize you with a cowl covering your head. If he does, then he will have a second story to tell. And *I* will be forced to explain to the seneschal and *visconte* why I skulked about in the company of a hunted criminal." He rubbed his thin hands together. "Ah well, I will soon speak with Janus. I must hear *his* tongue tell the story of finding Emeline. Though by now, he may have told it so often, he only recites the parts that gratify his listeners."

Bertwoin sped up his pace so they would get off the river path sooner. "What if Emeline really did go into the woods to meet someone?"

"A suitor? Sebastian the fletcher? It's possible, but young women tend to know who they can trust. The fact that she wasn't violated is suggestive. As we all know, rape is the greatest danger for any woman out alone. It has always been so. Jesus didn't send his female disciples out to preach because this danger existed even in His time."

"He had women disciples?"

"Oh yes, many. Mary Magdalene was chief among them. In fact, she was his favorite."

"Maybe the fire that burned Emeline belonged to the charcoalers," Bertwoin suggested, changing the subject.

The master bit his lip as he considered the idea. "An accident? Doubtful. They keep their fire banked." He sighed. "Though I also will need to talk with them. They may have seen someone in the forest."

"They are a secretive bunch."

"I often buy charcoal from them, so we are acquainted. They're no worse than most." The alchemist hummed. "But you are right. If they committed such a crime, they aren't likely to confess to having done so. Still, if they lie to me, I will feel it in my bones. We also have to consider Janus."

"Janus? Why would he kill her?"

"I do not know, but if he pretended to find her body, it would make him look innocent. And then there is the added benefit of it having brought him a fee."

"Where would *he* get a silver cross?"

"His sister, Na Thea, sells them."

Why had he not thought of that? The master seemed to consider everything.

Bertwoin pointed down the path toward the Devil's Doorstep. "A carpenter was hanged yesterday for breaking his apprentice's head open with a hammer."

"And broken open expertly, I'm sure. I'm told the apprentice enjoyed showing the carpenter's wife how to make a tight dovetail joint." The master chuckled at his own wit. "But I take your point. We will take another path and walk wide around the Devil's Doorstep. A murderous ghost with a ready hammer would be a formidable foe indeed."

The master scratched his beard. "Speaking of the carpenter's wife, it is possible that Emeline was murdered by a woman. Her beauty was intentionally marred. Do you know of any who feuded with her?"

Bertwoin shook his head. "Some women might have wanted to marry the fletcher or envied her, but I don't know of any who were jealous enough to torture and murder her. If Emeline had died by poison, that would have put a different face on this killer."

The master hummed agreement. "We will talk of this with Flowia. One of her duties is to listen to gossip." He turned onto a side path and peered into the mist where dawn lightened the horizon. "I doubt our murderer was female. I think I know his occupation. With luck, we will confirm this when we find where she was tortured."

How could the master know the killer's occupation? Bertwoin wanted to ask but hesitated to emphasize his ignorance. So he stayed quiet to keep the master's respect.

He crossed his arms over his chest, wanting more warmth from his wet cloak. How often had Mary Magdalene been uncomfortable when traveling? The master seemed to respect her as much as the Good Folk did.

"Don't take this as an insult," Bertwoin said. "But are you a true Christian of the Church?"

The master puckered his lips in thought. "Sometimes I ask myself that very question. I am a Christian. But my faith is ancient. I hark back to the days when Christianity had many sects before the Church chose only one path. That doesn't mean the other paths don't also lead to God."

"And you learned these secrets in the Holy Land?"

"Most of them. I knew many alchemists. Some were Muslims, others were Christians, and some called themselves Gnostics. The true alchemists attempted to purify their souls and reach toward God. I also met many who searched only for a way to make gold. They wanted to be rich in this world, not in the next one."

"I didn't mean to doubt you," Bertwoin apologized.

"I didn't take it as an insult, young plowman. It is a question you share with the bishop and abbot. You believe in ghosts, but you are also very much attuned to what you can see or touch or smell. I don't chide you for this. If fact, I welcome it. You don't let my ripe age or position stand in the way of your doubts. That's the main reason I insisted you come with me now. You won't let me fall into easy conclusions. This is as it should be, as long as you give me the respect I deserve for my age and experience."

They entered another pear orchard, its leaves trembling in the swirling breeze.

The master asked, "Do you know if this is a good place for picking blackberries?"

"It's not."

"Then we will look elsewhere."

The alchemist didn't stop until they came to the fallen willow where Janus had found Emeline's body. Bertwoin looked in the direction of the Devil's Doorstep, which lay less than a thousand paces from where they stood.

"You don't fear demons or other night things?" he asked.

"It's men I fear." He tapped Bertwoin's arm with his knuckles. "Is it not the same for you? Especially now that you are the stag the lawman hunts?"

"Me?" Bertwoin scanned the mist-filled woods. "I am wary of the *bayle* and the monks. But I can no more fight a devil than a wriggling worm can fight a crow."

"Then fight those you can. And if I were you, I would fear the clerics most. I have some influence with the *visconte* and seneschal and might persuade them to doubt your guilt enough to call their *bayle* to heel. But the abbot is another matter. It might be in his interest to have you hang for Emeline's death. And your trespass this night will anger him."

Bertwoin sighed. "I may have broken the nose of the brother who saw us."

"Trouble now seems attached to you like a shadow." The master gave him a musing look. "I do hope every day you hide in my house will not become an adventure. I prefer a life of quiet contemplation to one of noisy activity."

Bertwoin pulled the woolen cowl closer and watched for Janus, Guillaume the drowned-finder, or anyone else who might be about at this hushed hour of the morning.

The old man lifted his long face and appraised the dawn's faint glow in the hazy distance. "Day strides toward us. Let us see what it reveals. At least, the drizzle has stopped for a time."

He bent to study the ground and began shuffling in ever-widening circles. "So Janus found her here. But already too many have trampled the mud." He grunted in disgust. "A mob came to scratch the itch of their curiosity. Some of the sandal prints must come from the monks who carried her to the abbey. I think I see the *bayle's* print, but I cannot be certain. Other people besides him wear boots. If only our *bayle* had marked the soles of his boots with the sign of the Holy Cross, as some ex-crusaders do, we would recognize his coming and going."

Bertwoin smiled. Yes, it was like the proud *bayle* to cut crosses on his boots. He never tired of telling tales of his prowess while fighting in the far Levant.

The alchemist straightened and scanned the trees and shrubbery crowding down to the brown river. "She didn't run far. And she didn't run along the bank. With her chemise on fire, she was desperate to reach water. So it's a straight arrow's flight from here to where she was tortured. And her body probably didn't drift far before it hung up on the willow's branches. Let's enter the woods and walk north and south beside the river. If luck favors us, we will spy her track. We might even find her killer's footprints."

Just after sunrise, Bertwoin found a single footprint under a nettle tree. The print was petite enough to be Emeline's and showed only the toes and ball of a bare foot.

The master rushed over to examine it. "Well done, plowman, well done. It's the print of someone running toward the Aude. Yes, she raced straight as a mason's plumb-line to the water."

He ducked under a low limb and set a brisk pace away from the print toward the heart of the forest. He waved at the woods. "Plenty of blackberry bushes." After thirty paces, he stopped. "And what of this?"

He pointed to a natural rocky basin in a grove of lindens. Steep walls of limestone enclosed three sides of the pit, but the fourth wall sloped down into the cavity, making entry easy.

The master eyed the wide, natural depression. "Perfect. The murderer was fortunate indeed to find an invisible pit close to the river. Now we know the answer to our mystery of an unseen fire at night. The limestone walls here are high enough to hide the flame of a small blaze from anyone on the Aude's bank."

"And if anyone did see a glimmer in the woods here," Bertwoin added, "they might think it was a ghost or witches at their revels."

The old man chuckled. "Yes, and best left alone."

They crept down the sloping side with moss cushioning their steps. The cavity smelled of wet rock and fungi. A stately linden tree dominated the middle. The weeds at the base of this lone linden were blackened and shriveled by fire, as was the tree's rough trunk facing them.

"We have found where Emeline was tortured," the master whispered as if the spot were sacred. He pointed to a braided belt tossed aside in the weeds. "Hers, you think?"

"It's the type she wore on the day I saw her." Bertwoin remembered her dancing in the mud and swallowed to ease a sudden ache in his throat.

The master circled the regal tree. "No tunic, though. He must have carried it away with him."

"Why?"

"That is a mystery only he can answer." The alchemist circled the linden, then grunted as he squatted in front of the scorched place on the tree's trunk. He felt the ground with his fingertips. "The choppy mud here tells the story of her struggle. The bark behind the linden is scraped bare where she was tied with a rope. A thick rope." He shook his head as if to clear away a disturbing image. "My guess is he gagged her. Otherwise, the charcoalers or a night fisherman might have heard her screams."

"The fiend cut her face and her tongue," Bertwoin muttered.

The alchemist stood up. "Circle the pit. We now want to find *his* footprints."

As Bertwoin marched up and down the side of the pit

facing the Aude, he saw the master on his knees, examining the sloping side opposite him. This was the easy way to enter the basin, especially when carrying a body. Petite as she was, Emeline would still have weighed down the killer, but he doubted the alchemist would find any footprints in the spongy moss and crusty lichen. He might find a few skid marks. Probably, he—

Startled, Bertwoin stopped and squinted at the partial print of a sandal half-hidden under a spindly valerian plant. "Master," he called.

"That was quick work," the alchemist said. He squatted, brushed aside a cluster of hoverflies swarming over the valerian's flowers, and inspected the print.

"Well," Bertwoin said, "I looked in the direction of where I met Emeline first." He frowned. "This print points toward the basin. And no Emeline prints means he carried her, right?"

"Yes, the sandal's impression is deep." The alchemist's knee made a popping sound when he stood up again. "The bruise on Emeline's throat indicates that her attacker choked her, though not with his fingers. He probably strangled her with his arm until she fainted and carried her here. This is not so far as to be overly burdensome for the killer if we assume Emeline entered the woods near where you spoke with her."

The alchemist rubbed his beard as he scanned the ground for more footprints. "So now we know how he got her to the pit and why no one saw his fire. He probably kept it small. And the rope marks on the linden's bark show us that he tied her to the trunk." He closed his eyes a moment and bowed his head. "Verily, it is men we must fear most, young plowman. Not devils."

"How did she get loose?"

"Undoubtedly, she thrashed about while he cut her. She

was especially desperate when he lit a fire at her feet. Her writhing scraped the rope against the bark, and perhaps terror endowed her with wild strength. Somehow, she got loose. Somehow, she fought him off and fled to the Aude."

"With her gown aflame?"

"It might have only smoldered at first. Because of the rain, both her chemise and the firewood may have been wet. Her running blew it into full flame. Other than her feet and lower legs, her body shows little sign of being burned."

Bertwoin balled his hands into fists. "This was after the scurrilous cur slit open her nose, her cheeks, her chest, and sliced her tongue in half?"

"Yes. The fire came last. It is the usual end taken against females sentenced to death. No punishment is worse." The alchemist glanced around at the moist woods shining with mist. "So come, we will walk in the direction of where you talked with her."

They soon found her reed basket. The alchemist pointed to another sandal print and more disturbed mud. "This is where she was attacked and overpowered."

Bertwoin said, "She might have scratched his face when she fought him. My sisters fight that way."

"She might have."

"Brother Gregorius's face had gashes on it when we saw him at the abbey."

The alchemist hummed. "Yes, but I thought the cuts came from self-mutilation. They seemed too deep for mere scratch marks. Still, it bears looking into." He put a forefinger over his mouth as he considered an idea. "Tell me, does Agbart have many enemies?"

"A few. He's not an easy man to like."

"Do you know of any enemies angry enough to kill his only daughter in revenge?"

"Maybe. Tolarto hates him and is mean enough to do it.

Agbart has beaten the mule-headed bastard stupid at least twice. But Tolarto also fears Agbart. Flowia will know more about this than I do."

"Then we will ask her."

When they again reached the spot where Janus had fished Emeline out of the Aude, the master signaled for Bertwoin to stay in the sheltering woods and stepped out onto the narrow footpath. He made sure no one was in sight.

"It's time you returned to my house, plowman. Take care that no one sees you. I will continue to search here, then talk with Janus if I can find him. Isak the cloth merchant also needs to examine what I gleaned from under Emeline's fingernails. Go with God's protective hand over you, and remember what I said about Flowia. The less often you voice your opinion, the less often you will offend her."

CHAPTER X.

W hen Bertwoin came blinking out of the dark cellar into the kitchen after only four hours of sleep, Flowia met him posed like a shrew, her hand cocked on her hip.

She chanted,

> *"FinaUy is arisen our dawdler,*
> *after his agreeable sleep,*
> *and so our alehouse fuddler*
> *tosses morning on the dung heap."*

Like Emeline, Flowia sometimes rhymed her insults and her teasing, though unlike Emeline, she chanted rather than sang them. In this way, people with the wit for it copied the poets and jesters who engaged in flyting, the contests of arguing in rhymed insults. Of course, the people's verses were less polished.

Bertwoin ridiculed her barbed words with a yawn. "Maiden, your arrow misses the mark when you shoot at us."

Not seeing the master, he hoped the old man still lay abed. "Alehouse revelers don't work all night."

A little smile lifted Flowia's cheeks. "But, like you, the master toiled all night, didn't he?" she purred. "Yet he is still out seeking answers. And when he does return home, he'll not take repose before nightfall."

Bertwoin yawned again. Her banter entertained him and made their being alone together less awkward.

He flipped up a thumb to make a point. "Old men and women need less sleep. They no longer need rest to grow." He flipped up his forefinger to mark his second point. "I did the rowing and running last night, not the master." He saw the word "running" pique her curiosity and rejoiced at finding her weakness. He raised his middle finger for argument number three. "And why should I get up early? I have nowhere to go. The monks and the *bayle* hunt me like wolves slavering for meat." He flipped up a mischievous additional finger. "It's also possible the master sleeps elsewhere."

She snorted. "Ah, you don't know him."

"And you don't know where he is now or why he's gone there."

He smiled. Not only did she want to hear about last night, she also wanted to know where the master was at this moment. He waited to see what she would do next.

She glanced at the clay pot warming on her low hearth fire. "I hope pease porridge meets with your approval for breakfast. Oh, I mean luncheon."

He bowed as if thanking a noble lady. "Of course, it does. Pease porridge, along with more sleep, will put growth on me."

She served him porridge, wheat bread with honey, and brown ale at the kitchen table. Then Flowia busied herself with her limestone mortar, grinding dried leaves into a green powder. She kept glancing at him, waiting to hear of their adventures during the night, though she was too proud to beg him to tell the tale.

Bertwoin wasn't churlish. She had made him a delicious breakfast. So, while eating, he told her how they had sneaked into the cell where Emeline's forlorn body lay on a granite altar, of their escape from the abbey with the monks biting at their heels like a pack of eager hounds, and of their finding the scorched linden tree and Emeline's belt in the sunken limestone pit. He also added that the master had gone to show the cloth merchant scrapings taken from under Emeline's fingernails, and that afterward, the master intended to hear Janus repeat his story one more time.

The alchemist did indeed have stamina, and Bertwoin praised him for it. When Flowia understood that his compliments were genuine, she glowed with proud satisfaction.

She began humming a popular *canso* while crushing the leaves with her knobby pestle. When asked, she told him she was preparing the bitter motherwort to ease cramps and quickened childbirth.

Bertwoin lingered at the table, sipping the nutty ale she had given him. Rain pattered on the roof. It was a gentle summer, wet and warm, with the promise of a lavish grape harvest. The damp oak shingles above him scented the kitchen faintly with the ancient smell of a primitive forest. He felt as snug as a mouse tucked in its nest.

A man called a greeting from the poultry yard. Startled, Flowia and Bertwoin glanced at each other. Then she snatched his mug and plate off the table. Bertwoin darted into the cellar and hid behind its oak door with his ear pressed against it.

He heard Flowia greet the man at the front door and bring him into the kitchen. It sounded like Onfroi, a furrier who made a modest living from his shop in Castellar. He was known to be currently hunting for a wife.

Bertwoin moved his ear to the crack along the door's edge to hear better.

Flowia thumped a tankard on the table. "The master is absent at the moment."

"Yes, I met him earlier in town." Onfroi sounded more pleased by the master's absence than regretful.

So the furrier had come to visit Flowia when he knew the master wasn't at home. Bertwoin smiled. He would mention Onfroi's visit the next time Flowia twitted him. That would put a knot in her tail.

Flowia and Onfroi talked a bit about his furs, about her flourishing garden, and about the seneschal raising the price for grinding grain at the *visconte's* mill.

Then Flowia asked, "Has anyone seen the runaway plowman?"

"Hah, more than seen. Felt. Ox is a bold one," said the furrier, his voice full of respect. "Last night, a monk caught him in the abbey, probably stealing food. He—"

"It being night and the brother half asleep, how could he be certain it was the plowman and not just a prowling beggar?"

"Oh, but Ox woke him up. Smacked the black-robe on the nose and made him the monastery's martyr of the moment." Onfroi sighed loud enough for Bertwoin to hear. "He seems smart. But maybe he's like an ox in more ways than just size. I can't-"

> *"But they're useful, steady beasts,"* interrupted
>   Flowia,
> *"and take the yoke weU.*
> *They give us our harvest-feasts*
> *and mountains of manure as weU."*

Onfroi clapped. "True, but no one lauds an ox for its

brains. Why add the abbey black-robes to the pack hunting him? Were Agbart and the *bayle* not enough?"

"And monks do bring many benefits to our community," added Flowia, as if to blacken Bertwoin's brazen offense even more. "They feed the poor and shelter pilgrims and drain our marshes. Punching one seems capricious. Maybe he's like his father."

The furrier laughed. Bertwoin wasn't certain about the meaning of "capricious," but he knew it wasn't a compliment. Flowia was making a point of not defending him. Did she resent his bringing his problem to her beloved master and putting him in danger? After all, the alchemist wouldn't have been in the abbey last night if a certain Ox hadn't bulled into their lives. Or was she making sure Onfroi would never suspect that they were hiding Bertwoin?

"The monks are of good service," admitted Onfroi, "until their abbeys become rich, and they begin to wallow in luxury. It is written that the rich do not climb to heaven." After a pause, he added, "As for Ox, I saw Michel Azema sneaking about like a fox two days ago. Perhaps Bertwoin will go with him to tend sheep beyond the mountains. Fish of the same kind swim together."

"They're alike then?" Flowia said with some glee.

Bertwoin snorted. Oh yes, she knew he was listening.

"Michel doesn't deny killing my furrier friend while playing dice. But Bertwoin? He seemed as docile as the beast he's nicknamed for. Everybody wondered why the *bayle* suspected only him and didn't look at the charcoalers. But now some folks wonder how much violence sleeps in the plowman's breast. As you say, he is Clanoud's son."

"More ale?" Flowia asked.

"Please," said Onfroi. "It's excellent."

"We purchase it from the abbey."

Onfroi chuckled. "Another benefit from the monks. And

this tastes like their best brew, not the swill they give to beggars."

Bertwoin's mouth was beginning to feel dry. He was, of course, in the cellar and might help himself from a cask or barrel, but that would have been boorish. A guest should take only what the host or hostess chooses to give him.

After a moment of silence, Onfroi said, "You have a fine house here."

"It suits us."

"But do you not want a house of your own?"

Bertwoin smiled. Now that the small talk had prepared Onfroi's way, he intended to bargain for the article he had come to buy.

"I have what I want here," Flowia said, her tone now less friendly. "The master allows me my freedom."

"And children? They'll care for you when your bones ache and your muscles are stiff with age. And when you pass into the hand of God, you can know you added value to His world by leaving something of quality behind."

"Like an ermine leaves its valuable fur?"

Onfroi roared, a little too heartily. Was the strong ale making him overly gleeful? Or was he nervous?

"Just so," said the furrier. "But mark my words, when we meet again in the afterlife, you'll thank me for my counsel if you obey it."

"I'm not certain our souls will have the same home after death," Flowia quipped.

"Don't sell yourself short, maiden."

"I wasn't selling *myself* short."

Again, Onfroi roared. "Oh, have no fear for my soul. If need be, a Good Man will attend my death-bed and give me *consolamentum*. Then I can starve myself into heaven." The furrier coughed. "Before then, I do hope to have children of my own."

"You'll need a hen to lay the eggs."

Onfroi then gave Flowia a sermon on his virtues and what he could offer her. Bertwoin listened intently. Would he ever be able to offer as much as this furrier?

When Onfroi finished, Flowia asked, "And what of Jacquette? Her house expects you to take her for your wife."

"She is a fine woman and will make a fine wife. But I am a tradesman who wishes to better myself. A wife who can write will be valuable to me. Jacquette can't write, and her counting would never profit a merchant."

Flowia said brusquely, "The master taught me those skills to improve myself."

Bertwoin stood open-mouthed behind the door. He had heard that she could read words, but not that she could also reckon numbers. Everyone in his family could do normal counting, but none of them had learned to do the complicated accounting done by merchants.

Was the furrier saying he wanted to move beyond the role of a simple tradesman and become a merchant? And was Flowia's curt answer saying that marrying Onfroi would demean her learning?

"I bless the master for teaching you these skills. I'm good at what I do, and with your help and God's, we would prosper."

"I am content with my life here."

"Well, think on it. I have brought you a small keepsake."

After a pause, Flowia said, "Oh, this is too fine a gift for me."

"Not at all. Not at all. And remember, my life is not dull. Living with me would be an adventure." The bench moved. "I must be going now. Think more on it, if you value me at all."

When Bertwoin came out of the cellar, he found Flowia examining the stitching on a short fur blanket.

"Squirrel?" he asked.

"Yes. It's a fine piece." She refilled his mug with ale.

Bertwoin settled on the bench at the table. "Though you take me for a dawdler, I don't intend to just lounge about."

"Work will make time flow," she agreed.

"As long as I am where no visitors can see me."

"We have plenty of chores that can be done inside if you are willing to do women's work as well."

"My sewing is clumsy, but I can roast, grind, sweep, wash, and fetch."

"If you practice your sewing, you might make a good wife."

"Ah, but I'll always be a disappointment at having children."

"That won't—"

The heavy front door heaved open, and the master strode inside, carrying a hemp sack smelling of charcoal. For a moment's breath, Bertwoin resented the alchemist's intrusion into the cottage's quiet domesticity. It was as if the man had trespassed into his own house. Bertwoin silently chided himself for his ingratitude.

Flowia took the alchemist's woolen cloak and spread it over a pine chest to dry. Looking tired, the old man cut off a chunk of white goat's cheese, filling the kitchen with its milky odor, and sat down cross-legged on the floor instead of using a bench or stool. Flowia brought him red wine and fresh wheat bread.

The master chuckled. "I just met Onfroi not far down the path. He was whistling as if well pleased with himself. Said he would see me again soon." The alchemist glanced slyly at the fur blanket Flowia held. "So he's interested?"

"He pretends to be."

The master glanced at Bertwoin before refocusing his curiosity on Flowia. "Pretends? How so, daughter?"

"Onfroi schemes more than a king. He's a *credente*, though

he hides this by being jocular about the Good Folk and calling out their faults. Visiting me as if he wanted to take a Christian wife disguises his true religious beliefs. Also, he'll make certain Jacquette's family knows that she has competition. They may then find it wise to raise her dowry."

"Really?" Bertwoin asked. "He seemed convincing when he pleaded his offer."

Flowia blew out her breath, dismissing the furrier's performance. "Men often promise moonlight and honey. Women then have to make do with oil lamps and stinging bees."

Bertwoin tried to remember how much he had bragged about himself.

The alchemist sat hunched, his face drawn. He shook his head. "You do look upon us with distrust, daughter."

"I'm rarely disappointed in my opinion. Not all men are as truthful as you."

The alchemist nodded toward Bertwoin. "Our plowman is lauded for his generosity."

She gave him a curt nod. "Yes, he is." A sly smile crept onto her face.

> *"He is known to give aU*
> *to the ones who give him a caU.*
> *He donated a blow to a monk's nose*
> *which now resembles a bright red rose."*

The master's face became solemn. "A sin he committed to save me."

"But the reason you were inside the abbey was to save me," Bertwoin reminded him.

"True, but also to save young women from torture and death." The alchemist pointed his dagger at Flowia's limestone mortar. "The people expect me to pour quicksilver into that vessel and see the evil face of Emeline's murderer revealed there."

Flowia glanced at Bertwoin's expression and told the master, "Someone else thought to find such magic in you."

The alchemist laid his dagger on his thigh. He pretended to pour quicksilver into his cupped hand and stared at a palm discolored by chemicals. "I see Emeline on the Aude's bank. She carries a reed basket for berries and mushrooms and is talking to a sturdy plowman." The master gazed at Bertwoin and waited for the details.

Bertwoin shrugged. "We met by chance on the path, as I said. I was carrying a sickle to my Uncle Roland so he could repair its handle."

The alchemist nodded. "And how long did you stay with your uncle?"

"Ah, I didn't go. Instead, I went in search of Tolarto, who had seen me and slipped away into the woods. He owed me a debt at the time. I never found him. Anyway, I decided to visit Uncle Roland on some other day, because it would be long after dark before I returned home."

"Pity. Your uncle might have saved your neck. Ah well, then it is still up to us to prove you innocent." He scratched his beard. "Janus confirmed that Emeline was wearing a silver cross when he found her. So we know the brothers at the abbey didn't put it on her corpse. Could she have repented her belief in the Good Folk and returned to the Church?"

"No," Flowia told him. "Or at least, she hadn't altered her beliefs three days before market day. I met her as she and Gertrude were going to hear two Good Men preach."

"Then her killer placed it on her. Why? Ridicule? Or did her murderer wish to keep demons away from her corpse?" He lowered his eyebrows and looked accusingly at Flowia. "Some folk would do well to be more careful about the company they keep. The Church is jealous of its power and guards its faith like a father guards his daughter's virginity."

"I remain in the Church," Flowia argued, regally defiant, "but I think the Good Folk have merit too."

Bertwoin wanted to turn the conversation away from religion before they fell into blasphemy. "You saw guilt on Prior Simon's face," he said to the master.

"I did, but I believe something else causes this guilt. Prior Simon is known to tolerate the Good Folk and even some of their heretical beliefs. He isn't given to torturing young women." The master stretched and yawned. "Now, as for the abbot, who can say?"

Shocked, Bertwoin snorted. Flowia shook her head at his overreaction and told him, "He's just being provocative."

The alchemist picked up his Moorish dagger, its blade smeared with goat cheese, and waved it about. "Oh, am I? Often, I think I see a mote of murder in the abbot's left eye."

Flowia's look pitied the master as if he were as naïve and blind as a newborn puppy. "Maybe this murderous hate comes into his eye when *you* arrive. It then ebbs when *you* leave."

The alchemist threw his head back and guffawed. "Ah well, I also met and spoke with Brother Theodoric. He told me Brother Gregorius had mutilated his young face, as we saw it at the abbey, to atone for the sin of pride." The master shook his head, his expression disbelieving. "He used a cursed knife. So his wounds festered. No doubt, this extra punishment pleased him. He also burned his hand to demonstrate his faith. Just keeping this saintly boy alive robs Brother Theodoric of many precious hours."

Flowia crimped her lips in disgust. "He craves an early death and martyrdom." She glanced at the hemp sack the master had carried in. "What of the charcoalers?"

"Ah yes, those who remain unseen. Possible suspects, but only if they committed the murder together." The master saw

Bertwoin eying his sack and explained, "I use it in my work-shop, and Flowia uses charcoal as a remedy against some poisons."

The old man took a slow sip of his red wine. "Anyway, only two charcoalers are working there at present, and since they must keep constant watch over the fire, one sleeps while the other remains awake. The one guarding their work might have sneaked away and caught Emeline, but he couldn't have tarried for long. And I think our torturer acted with deliberate slowness."

Flowia hissed in a breath.

"Yes," said the alchemist. "Of course, they might have done it together. But why? She wasn't defiled. And they would have had to be watching and waiting for her. She was attacked soon after she entered the woods."

"Why not after she had finished picking blackberries and was leaving the forest?" Bertwoin asked.

"There were only morels in her basket, no blackberries." The master drank some more wine, then yawned. "I also learned that Brother Nigellus has already fixed his holy zeal on another young woman. Now that Emeline is beyond redemption, Roqua's wayward soul merits his full attention."

Flowia's mouth hung open a moment. "Gertrude's daughter? Does he think he can shorten the ears of a rabbit or make a pig dance?"

The alchemist clapped his hands in delight. "Yes, the dove means to hunt the hawk."

Bertwoin hoped Roqua beat his sanctimonious accuser with a long wooden spoon. She was the type to do so. "Did Janus say anything more?"

"He says Emeline's body was rigid. So her death was still fresh upon her. The killer may have captured her just after she left you and the monks. But who knows how long she was tied to the linden in the pit?"

"Oh." Flowia scooped water from a copper pan into her cupped hand and splashed it on her face.

The alchemist sighed. "Yes, it's horrible to imagine. But this may have given her time to scrape the rope binding her wrists against the tree's trunk and shred it. So before he could burn her, she was able to free herself and flee."

Bertwoin growled, "Her struggles brought her little profit, though drowning is less painful than burning. Did she swoon when she reached the river, or did the piss-bucket catch her and drown her like an unwanted pup?"

Bertwoin heard Flowia sob behind him. A knot of sorrow also clogged his chest.

The solemn alchemist stared down at the rushes on the floor. "More likely her tormentor drowned her. The use of water suited his purpose as well as fire."

"And Isak?" Flowia asked, moving their conversation to an easier subject. "Bertwoin said you went to talk with him."

"He could not be certain if a bit of thread under her fingernails was wool or hemp or flax. We couldn't even determine its true color." The old man took a deep breath. "Ah well, let us move to my laboratory."

Flowia asked, "Then you will not be going to bed?"

"No, daughter. Work will clear my thoughts and ease my mind."

"I told Bertwoin that you could work all night and all day. Unlike him."

"You are too hard on our guest, little sparrow. Younger animals require more sleep. Crusty, old dogs like me need less rest and have less trouble delaying it."

Bertwoin grinned at her.

CHAPTER XI.

I n his crowded workshop, the alchemist sat as solemn as an owl beside a bulbous glass vessel with a small blaze under it. The firelight bounced the red coloring of his robe onto his lean face, while green liquid boiled inside the cucurbit's bulging belly. The liquid steamed into a mist that flowed through a long glass tube, ending in a copper pot with a sealed lid. Bertwoin pumped a small leather bellows to make the fire hotter.

Seeing his keen interest, the old master smiled. "The mist turns to liquid again when it cools, but it will then be as pure as an angel's heart. If only we could burn away our own sins so easily. A Jewess named Maria invented this process more than a thousand years ago."

"What does this magic liquid do when it's pure?"

Flowia rolled her eyes at his childlike belief in magic. "I use it to make a lotion that steals pain from joints and muscles."

The liquid's brisk cedar scent filled the workshop. Bertwoin breathed deeply and let its prickly vapor, which cooled his nostrils, clear his head. He felt trusted and a little honored at being allowed to work the bellows and watch the master practice his art.

A pebble hit a wooden shutter. Someone outside coughed. Flowia frowned at the door, clearly wanting to finish pulping leaves, fir needles, and purple berries into a medicinal paste. She looked at the master.

The person outside coughed again. Bertwoin saw no place for him to hide.

In answer to Flowia's questioning look, the master nodded. She set her work aside and stomped to the front door.

Bertwoin caught a glimpse of Roqua, Gertrude's eldest daughter, as Flowia slipped outside and closed the door behind her. He hadn't realized Roqua would be standing where he could see her and hoped she hadn't caught a glimpse of him.

She was a young widow, who had a cobbler as a suitor. He was a *credente* whose wife had run off with a traveling acrobat and was now eager to marry Roqua because he had two small children in need of a mother.

Brother Nigellus was also now interested in her, though maybe not in the same way. And as Flowia had said, saving Roqua's heretical soul would be a punishing climb up a rocky slope for the little monk. Her mother, Gertrude, was the well-known Good Woman who had been Emeline's mentor.

Outside, Roqua told Flowia, "I cut my finger and it's festering."

The master got up, huffing a bit as he did so, and shuffled to the door. Bertwoin moved to where Roqua could not see him when the alchemist stepped outside.

Bertwoin judged the fire's dance. It flamed lively enough for now, and since the copper pot had already swallowed almost all of the green liquid, the fire no longer needed to breathe heavily. So he left his work and crept to a front shutter and peeked through the crack between two slats. People normally kept their shutters open during the day to let in air and sunlight, but to guard his secrets, the master always kept those on his workshop closed.

Outside, Flowia asked, "And how goes your man trouble?"

Roqua coughed and said, "Ah, the cobbler is no trouble. He's not a love-sick flea like your furrier."

Flowia hummed and smiled in the superior way of one who knows another's secret. "I was speaking of a certain monk."

Roqua looked aghast and then disgusted. "He's like a louse," she boomed. "His pesky attention causes me to itch. If only I could crush Brother Nigellus between my thumbnails and be rid of him for good."

The master teased, "It does not flatter you that he singled you out and practices his trade on you?"

Roqua crossed her arms under her breasts. "I think he chooses to save the daughter from eternal hellfire to wound the saintly mother."

Her eyes widened and lit up. "Speaking of saints, have you heard that Brother Gregorius had another vision? Saint Nazarius appeared to him again. The abbot is drunk with joy, and the bishop is as green as old cheese with envy. None of his priests fall down in trances. I doubt Brother Gregorius has to clean any privy closets now."

"Ah," Flowia said, "but he may demand to do so. Many saints in the past performed loathsome tasks to debase themselves." She smiled mischievously. "So, have you taken up self-mutilation too?"

Roqua snorted and held up a forefinger wrapped in hemp cloth, its weave darkened by dried blood. "Brother Gregorius wants sainthood, not me. I sliced it while cutting up a chicken, and it festers like a punishment." She scowled at her injured finger as if it had been naughty. "I need you to nurse it back to health."

Flowia pointed to a tree stump. "Sit there, and I'll tend to it." She hurried toward the cottage.

Bertwoin realized that for Roqua, Flowia was the important person to see. The alchemist, of course, knew how to brew medicines, but it was Flowia who applied them. She also made a number of salves and ointments herself. After all, it was she who grew the necessary herbs in her garden or picked them in the forest and ground them into powders. It was she who had learned the healing arts from Na Thea and other wise women.

The alchemist stood off to one side, warming himself in the sun like a thin, red lizard. "What do you hear of Emeline's murder?"

Roqua perked up. She knew when anyone in Montredon burped, and she was ever willing to tell of it.

"I hear many things," she said, her smile sly and mocking. "Bertwoin the plowman is away to the mountains, or he now lives with his widowed aunt and plows fields for her, or he has run off to be a charcoaler." She studied the master, waiting to see his reaction.

"You think he murdered Emeline?" he asked.

"Ox? He's more likely to save a woman than to kill one." She glanced at the master's workshop and smiled. "I'm surprised he didn't run to you. He's the type who believes you could conjure up the name of Emeline's murderer for him. He might offer to trade plowing for your magic."

Bertwoin's face flushed warm. Did everyone think he was as gullible and half-witted as Hilario? And her sly smile bothered him. Had she seen him when Flowia opened the workshop's door?

The master bowed to her. "Your reasoning has merit. If he did come to me, though, I would use knowledge instead of magic to prove him innocent."

Flowia flounced out of the cottage carrying a knife with a small, curved blade, two strips of cloth, a pine box, and a small copper pan. She strode to the stump, laid everything except the pan beside Roqua, then marched to the tiny spring.

"You don't believe Ox killed her, do you?" Roqua asked the master.

"No, though I think he is strong enough to carry her body."

"So you think she was killed by a man? Someone strong?"

Flowia hurried back with her pan half full of cold water, probably not wanting to miss any of the conversation. She too thrived on gossip.

"Yes," said the master, smoothing his beard. "There are plenty of strong women, but I think the killer was a man, someone young who lives apart from others, maybe not physically, but morally. He is also local."

Flowia unwrapped Roqua's swollen finger and peeled away the hemp strip crusted with blood. From where he stood, Bertwoin could see the wound clearly. Roqua had sliced open the second joint of her left forefinger, the wound an angry red with yellow lips. Part of the new scab had come off with the cloth, so the cut began to seep white pus.

Roqua asked, "So it wasn't someone who came here to trade, or a shepherd like Michel? I saw him lurking about. He and Emeline once made dove eyes at each other before Agbart put a stop to it."

Flowia opened the cut farther with her keen knife. Roqua didn't flinch and watched Flowia work as if the infected finger didn't belong to her.

The master said, "Someone like Michel is possible. He was local and might know of the pit where she was tortured."

Roqua looked sorrow-stricken, her face pale and tight at the mention of Emeline's torture.

Flowia squeezed pus from the wound and washed the inflamed finger in the copper pan. "Why Emeline?" she asked.

"Exactly," the alchemist said. "Why her and why then? Was she just unfortunate and easy prey for a depraved killer who happened upon her? Or," he asked Roqua, "was this crime committed because the killer hated her for being a *credente* of your creed? Or did he hate her for being a pretty young woman? He did mutilate her face and cut her soft breast."

Flowia's face was rigid with hatred as she wrapped green leaves around Roqua's clean finger.

Roqua inspected the wrapping. "I've seen this plant."

"It's called woundwort." Flowia bound the leaves to the wound with a thin strip of linen. "If it doesn't start to heal in three days, come see me."

"Thanks, Flowia." She held up her bandaged finger. "I'll bring you grain and a basket of woundwort for this." She tilted her head to one side and glanced at the workshop. "If I find the plowman, I'll give you the denier instead."

Flowia raised her eyebrows. "A denier?"

Roqua put her fist to her mouth and coughed into her hand. "Oh, you don't know, do you?" she said with the glee of one who knows a secret. "Agbart will pay one lovely silver denier to the person who tells him where Ox is hiding."

For a breath, Bertwoin felt as if he were falling. Now even children would hunt for him.

"And guess who's looking hardest for him? Tolarto," she cried without waiting for an answer. "He's running about as sprightly as a squirrel with its tail on fire."

There was an awkward moment of silence, and Bertwoin knew Roqua's quip about the squirrel reminded them, as it did him, of Emeline running to the river with the bottom of her chemise on fire.

"He's made finding the plowman his new trade," Roqua said. "He needs a new trade. No one will hire him. He'd steal the breath from a baby." She laughed harshly. "Yet he comes to hear *maman* preach and professes to follow our ways."

She turned to Flowia. "Many thanks for the rose ointment you brought for my sister's body." Her voice became hoarse with grief. "*Maman* praised your kindness to everyone. You should join us. You're too good for the Church."

"I need no thanks," Flowia said.

Roqua bit her lip and sucked air in through her teeth. "If I wanted to find her killer," she told the master, "I'd look at Sebastian's brother, Villenc. The stonebreaker curses and rages against us. Our beliefs insult him. He even refuses to sit on a bench if he learns that a Good Man or Good Woman sat there before him. He threatened to blind Emeline."

The alchemist nodded. "He's strong enough and is no friend to women. Does the stonebreaker keep company with them?"

"He's mostly seen with men," Roqua said in a tone that suggested he was a fool. "But then that's true of many men."

"Some monks are crazy with religion," Flowia suggested. "They don't live alone, but many are young and local, and many consider women unclean and evil."

The master hummed. "Whoever killed Emeline had a surfeit of time during the night to torture her. Monks must be present every few hours for night prayers, and their absence is both noticed and punished. A priest would have more opportunity."

Roqua laid a hand against her breastbone, coughed twice,

and stood up. "May the good god bless you both and all that you do."

"I'll walk a little way with you," Flowia told her. "I have a favor to ask."

Bertwoin hurried to the bellows and pumped them a few times before the master bustled back inside. The alchemist sat on a stool and stared at a wall, thinking.

When Flowia finally reentered the workshop, Bertwoin said, "There's talk of her marrying the cobbler."

She shook her head. "*His* house agrees to it, but not the house *she* lives in. Roqua brought too many sheep and geese with her when she married."

Bertwoin nodded. It was a common problem: if Roqua left her husband's brothers, her dowry went with her.

Still frowning, the master glanced at Flowia. "Did you talk with Roqua about her cough?"

"Yes, she is not yet spitting up blood, but she soon will be." Flowia bowed her head, closed her eyes, and sighed. "Poor Gertrude. All her children seem fated to die before her. Little Marthe is also sick now."

"The priest preaches that this is her punishment from God," Bertwoin said. "The bishop and abbot both say she brought this trouble down on her own head when she left the Church."

"Just like Job's wife," Flowia grumbled. "Blameless Gertrude loses all her children. Maybe the Good Folk are right. Maybe an evil god does rule over our world."

Bertwoin made the sign of the cross to protect them all from her blasphemy.

"Is anything wrong?" Flowia asked the master, who scowled at a closed front shutter.

"It's probably just my imagination, but Roqua kept glancing at the workshop as if she knew Bertwoin was hiding here. We may have been foolish."

"Even if she saw him here, she would never tell on him."

"She would never knowingly do so, but secrets have a way of coming out." He snapped his fingers. "Ah well, no matter. Bertwoin has only nine days here before a carter leads him away to the mountains."

CHAPTER XII.

For six days, they made no progress on finding Emeline's killer because the master had to accompany the *visconte* to Béziers to help settle a dispute.

So during this time, Flowia worked Bertwoin like a kitchen drudge. She also decided that now was a favorable time to build shelves in the cellar for her herbs and supplies. Bertwoin spent large portions his days and nights underground in the cellar.

He was relieved when the master returned three days before a carter was due to lead him up into the mountains. Now he would get a day or two of rest, and they would again work on solving Emeline's murder.

At the kitchen table, the alchemist opened a piece of linen and inspected the residue he had scraped from under Emeline's fingernails.

Dissatisfied, he grunted and said to Flowia and Bertwoin, "If only Isak could have helped me."

The master took a round lens not much larger than a silver coin from his leather pouch and used it to magnify the scrapings. "I showed him this, some dirt and a strand that's little more than a hint of a thread. Is it from a cloak or a tunic? Is it wool or flax? If only I could coax this mulish clue into telling its tale."

He brought the cloth and magnifying glass closer to his eye. "I say dirt, but Isak pointed out that it's granular. Maybe tree bark? Did she break her fingernails while scraping the rope against the linden?"

"Might the thread be hemp instead of wool?" asked Flowia.

"Hemp?" The master stared at the underside of his shingle roof as he considered her question. "Yes, of course. She may have clawed at the rope that bound her wrists. But that brings us no closer to finding her murderer. And I must shun my habit of accepting easy answers. I assumed the debris was dirt and the strand was wool."

The master glanced at the door, then at Bertwoin. "I will now go talk with Prior Simon and judge whether he's your ally or your foe. Then I will visit our *bayle* and explain to him that you are not a rabid wolf but a sheep of the flock."

"A docile ox?" Flowia suggested.

The master waggled his hands back and forth. "Maybe. A certain monk with a swollen nose might argue against his being docile. But your underlying argument has merit, daughter. Our plowman here is not some wild beast stalking the forest, but neither is he a flock animal."

Bertwoin took a sip of the bitter herb tea Flowia served him every morning. It tasted like a dunghill smelled. She claimed it enlivened him and made him eager to work. He wondered if she served it to him as a prank, just to laugh at him as he drank this swill. He took another hesitant sip to be polite. Maybe he was a tame ox.

It heartened him to know that both Flowia and the alchemist believed he was innocent. He hoped, however, that they didn't believe he was as slow-witted as a sheep or an ox.

Bertwoin mumbled, "I think of myself more as a horse, a worthy steed, than a wooly sheep."

"Not as a charging ox?" Flowia asked, barely suppressing her laughter.

He shrugged. "Better a plow-puller than a bottom-bumping toad or a soul-stealing owl."

The master pressed a hand against his lower back and stretched. He shook his head in disagreement. "The owl was once the symbol of the goddess of wisdom." He stared at the rushes strewn across the cottage floor, his expression musing. "Ah well, the golden days ruled by familiar gods are long gone."

Was the old alchemist lamenting the passing of pagan times? Did he truly believe those gods were real and once ruled over men?

The master stood without speaking, wheezing a little. Flowia had told Bertwoin that many alchemists died from coughing sicknesses. The vapors in their workshops ate away their lungs. The powders they used and the metals they handled also addled their wits, turning them into fools like Hilario.

The master shook his head as if coming awake. "Anyway, it's imperative for the *bayle* to question Brother Nigellus about the evidence he presented against you. Why does he accuse you? We must turn the *bayle* loose on the scent of the *real* killer."

The old man's phlegmy laugh sounded more regretful than happy. "Ah, maybe I *should* pretend to see all of this reflected in a puddle of quicksilver. It would please the people. Unfortunately, the *bayle* is too worldly to believe in magic. That's as it should be. If unleashed and pointed in the right direction, he is the hound to flush out the cur that savaged young Emeline."

Flowia groaned. "And what of poor Gertrude? She didn't

need this sorrow too. She lost two daughters to the spitting-blood disease, and little Marthe is now sick. Roqua seemed all she had left."

Confused, Bertwoin frowned. "What? Roqua too? She was here just six days ago."

"Yes," the master said, "I told Flowia that I met Gertrude carrying cloth to sell in town yesterday. Roqua never returned to her own house and hasn't visited her mother either, as is her habit. No one has seen her since the day after Flowia dressed her cut finger."

"Oh, no," Bertwoin said. "Not again."

The alchemist bowed his head. "Maybe Roqua fled to Catalonia with a lover, as some young women do. But it is foolish to think so. She's not the type to abandon her grieving mother. So, before I question the prior, I must talk with Gertrude. She may know something that will help us."

Flowia sighed, then pointed to a joint of pork hanging from a sooty roof beam. "Let's give her a cut of pig meat for little Marthe," she said in a hoarse voice. "We can make do with half of what we have here."

The alchemist disagreed with a shake of his head. "Give it all to me. We can make do with dried fish and beans. And give me a portion of dried fish for her to eat," he added, since Gertrude wasn't allowed to eat meat or cheese.

Flowia praised him with a look. Her love for the master was as apparent to Bertwoin as the kitchen table. He too felt honored to witness the master's unsparing charity.

Bertwoin remembered the master saying that the fiend would kill again. "So if it is as I think," he said, "we know where we must look to find Roqua."

The master closed his eyes and mumbled a quick prayer. "Yes, and I fear what we may find there. We will visit the pit after nightfall when you can come with me."

"Roqua is twice as strong as Emeline," Flowia said, snatching at hope's retreating tail.

The alchemist patted her shoulder. "Yes, little sparrow, but our murderer will have learned much from his first kill. He is now better at doing evil."

Bertwoin scowled. "If we do find Roqua's corpse, the *bayle* will ask how you knew where to look. The pit is well hidden in the deep forest."

"Yes, he is suspicious of all the wrong people, isn't he?" The master sucked in his bottom lip for a moment. "We will see if he accepts the truth as his answer. I will tell him murderers often copy their successes. So, I searched the woods near where Janus found wretched Emeline. Let other folks believe I used magic."

After the master left to visit Gertrude, Bertwoin found that Flowia was in a snappish mood and was not overly pleased with his company. So he retreated to the alchemist's workshop. There he sat on a three-legged stool in a corner and began to braid a fish trap.

Tonight, he and the master would be busy. Tomorrow night, he would sneak down to the Aude and sink one or two traps in the river. He would check them before sunrise while darkness still cloaked him.

After he left to tend sheep in mountain pastures, Flowia could see to the traps. The fish they caught was his way, along with the plowing he would do, of thanking the master for proving him innocent.

Bertwoin had just finished the first trap when he heard Flowia yell at someone. Shocked, he crept to the front window, pushed the shutter open a thumb's width, and peeked outside.

Flowia stood in front of the cottage's doorway, blocking four monks in black robes and two robust laymen from invading her home. Both guards and one monk carried cudgels. Had Roqua seen him and talked, as the master said she might?

Flowia, of course, knew enough not to provoke the brothers or laymen by drawing her knife. It was better to let the guards roughly shove her aside and invade her empty house.

Bertwoin looked behind him. The workshop had no back door, and the window in the rear wall was just large enough for a six-year-old boy to slip through it. No man could thread that needle. Why had he let himself be trapped like a fish?

Cornering their quarry in the workshop gave full advantage to the monks. And some of them might even take grim pleasure in having an excuse to smash the master's equipment.

Bertwoin touched the hilt of his knife and decided not to draw it. What good would it do to prove he was innocent of murdering Emeline, then hang at the Devil's Doorstep for killing a brother or one of the laymen guards? Besides, it wasn't in his nature. When it came to killing, he was more like an ox than a fox.

His only choice, then, was to run for it. He slipped out of his clogs and kicked them aside. One of the smaller monks might catch him, but he doubted the burly guards could outrun him. Few men could.

He peeked outside again. A haughty little monk and a hefty layman guard with a scar across his left eye had left the group and marched toward the workshop. His only chance now was to surprise them.

Bertwoin flung the door open right in their faces. The monk's eyes widened in fear. The guard blocked his path and thrust the end of his cudgel at his belly. Bertwoin flinched sideways, and the club's head bounced off his ribs instead of punching his stomach. Still, the blow had the force of a mule's kick. Pain paralyzed him for half a breath, and he grabbed his side and leaned into the hurt to relax his rib muscles.

"Leave him be," Flowia yelled.

The guard with a knife slash across his left eye glared at him.

Gritting his teeth, Bertwoin rammed his shoulder at the man's chest. The guard pushed against him with his empty hand and softened the power of his lunge. He also backed away, further weakening the attack.

Bertwoin straightened, and as he did so, he swung his fist at the guard's jaw. The movement wrenched the injured muscles near his bruised ribs, causing him to cry out in pain and weakening the force of his blow.

The burly guard ducked toward him, and his fist hit the man's skull just above his left ear.

Bertwoin cried out. It felt as if he had smacked a stone wall. He flapped his hand to shake the pain out of his knuckles.

For a moment, the guard's eyes were vacant. Then he shook his head to clear it.

The monk who had accompanied the guard whacked Bertwoin across the back of his head with his club. Far away, Bertwoin heard a woman scream.

He fell to his knees in front of the workshop, his arms folded over his throbbing head. Bent double, he began rocking to relieve his pain.

A shadow fell over Bertwoin, and he stared down, his vision blurry, at a monk's sandals and dusty feet. Somehow, he realized the brother had stretched an arm above his head to protect him. In a faraway voice, he heard the monk say, "Don't knock him out."

He had failed to bring down the guard. He wasn't the fighter his father was. He never would be.

"Unless you want to carry him," the monk said, his voice now sounding less distant.

"Carry him?" the guard said. "I'll kill him and leave him here for the dogs and pigs."

"The abbot wishes him alive. Don't make him unable to confess."

"He'll pay for hitting me," the guard muttered.

The wooden toe of the guard's clog kicked Bertwoin's forearm, which was wrapped around his pounding head. He yelped. Pain radiated along his arm.

"Forgiveness is divine," the brother sniveled, his tone irritating even Bertwoin.

The guard growled like a savage dog. "Tell that to the abbot, monk."

"Watch your tongue, churl, or you might share his cell."

"He'd be better company than a black-robed, prick-tugger like you." The guard strode away.

"Get him up," the monk ordered.

Feet appeared around him, and hands grabbed Bertwoin's arms. Someone slipped his knife out of its sheath. He heard Flowia say near him, "He doesn't leave here until I've seen to his wounds."

"You've no say in this, harlot," the lead monk shouted. "You and your heathen alchemist will answer to the abbot for his presence here. Now get back inside your house before we take *you* with us."

CHAPTER XIII.

Bertwoin convulsed like a puking dog when they lifted him to standing, and his legs seemed no stronger than blades of grass. He tasted stomach acid in his throat but fought down the urge to vomit.

No, the eldest son of Clanoud would not shame himself even when the wavering ground and dizzy sky and black-robed monks whirled around him. An eye-watering ache throbbed through his skull.

Merciful Jesus, help me.

The two guards held him still while a brother bound his wrists tight behind him. The guards then began to half-walk, half-lug him over uneven ground. Flashes of light blazed and died behind his closed eyes.

"Wait," he pleaded, and the guards stopped. Bertwoin blinked, surprised they had obeyed him.

The monk in charge barked, "Come on, peasants. Why do you tarry? The abbot wants him taken to the palace *now.*"

His arrogant expression and tone were so smug, so indignant and self-righteous, Bertwoin wanted to hit him. That's what he was good at, wasn't it? He had a talent for smacking monks on the nose. But now those who prayed, those who claimed to serve a merciful God, would punish him.

"Then let the bishop come and haul him to his palace in St. Vincent's," the guard muttered.

"The abbot will hear of your disobedience, churl. Now, let's be off."

The unsympathetic monk turned and marched away. Neither of the guards moved. A brother shoved the squint-eyed layman from behind. The guard let go of Bertwoin's arm and faced the monk, who backed away.

Unexpectedly left holding Bertwoin's weight by himself, the smaller guard tottered half a step sideways, jerking Bertwoin, who had to clamp his throat against the shameful urge to vomit.

Scar-eye grabbed the front of the monk's woolen robe and hauled him closer. "Shove me again, make-believe holy man, and I'll lay you out like a corpse." He raised a forefinger and turned it in a circle to indicate the other monks. "Then your brothers will learn what a burden it is to carry *you*. And they'll not thank you for it."

There was an awkward moment when even the arrogant brother in charge was silent. Bertwoin stared at a dunghill as tall as his shoulder, trying to focus and settle his whirling sight.

"Where are you taking me?" he mumbled.

The small guard holding his left arm, who smelled of ale, snickered. "To luxury, peasant, to luxury. There's a snug nest waiting for you under the bishop's palace."

Even a dungeon's damp cell was now welcome to Bertwoin. He yearned like a lover to lie on a dead-still, stone floor under the bishop's elegant palace.

How could these monks and their toady guards expect him to march all the way to the Toulouse Road, cross the river at the wooden bridge, and stumble through noisy St. Vincent?

"I won't make it," he told them.

"You walk, murderer," Scar-eye muttered as he grabbed Bertwoin's arm, "or we'll drag you by your ankles, bumping your head over the rocks and ruts. Let's see how you enjoy that."

They began the punishing hike with the haughty little monk striding in front of them. The guards strained to support Bertwoin, and the remaining three black-robed brothers crowded behind him. No doubt, they wanted to be well away from the house before the alchemist returned. None of them knew what dark magic the master might call down on their cowled heads.

But the blow to his skull had crippled Bertwoin's balance. After he had staggered twenty or thirty paces, he fell to his knees. The guards cursed and hauled him to his feet again, wrenching his injured ribs. Pain speared through his chest like a knife thrust.

Bertwoin purposely studied the problem of his pain to distance himself from it, as if though encased in his body, he was detached from its suffering.

He stumbled along, letting the laymen lug most of his weight. He punished them as much as he could, but he made certain he stayed upright. Falling hurt too much. It twisted his damaged ribs and snapped his throbbing head.

The pear-shaped guard who smelled of ale jabbed his injured ribs with a thumb, breaking his concentration. Bertwoin nearly fainted. They lurched sideways as the guards fought to keep him upright.

Scar-eye snarled and shouted, "Fool! Let him be. We can't carry him the whole damned way."

Bertwoin stood panting, his head lolling, his chin against his chest. Why was God punishing him like this? He had sinned no more than most and even less than many, especially those like the greedy bishop, who worshiped power and wallowed in wicked luxury, who slept on silk and rode a fine white stallion. Why should he, an innocent plowman, shuffle toward a dingy cell under a palace? Today, the Devil danced and cackled in delight.

It was said the cruel bishop enjoyed hearing the delicious screams of his prisoners. Did their groans make him revel in his sweet holiness? It was said he often witnessed their torture, as if his presence added dignity to the dislocating of their joints.

When Bertwoin glanced back toward the master's cottage, he saw Flowia gliding along at a safe distance behind them. Her long hair was modestly gathered at the back of her head in a white linen coif. As always, she held her dress hem up with one hand and seemed to skim rather than tread the ground.

Yes, she had to warn the master of the monks' coming and Bertwoin's arrest. The wily alchemist needed to hatch an answer to the charge of sheltering a criminal. Once again, the *visconte* would have to protect his wayward goldsmith.

So the master and Flowia were now in peril because of him.

Walking quickened his blood flow and made his head thump like a minstrel's drum. He contemplated fate's slow steps. Oh, if only he had stayed in the master's cottage instead of going to the workshop. But he hadn't wanted Flowia to see him weaving the fish traps. The gift of them was to be a surprise. Besides, if she had seen him weaving reeds, she would have insisted that he do it her way, not his.

When their group finally reached the wooden bridge crossing the Aude, Scar-eye said, "We stop here a moment."

The guards let Bertwoin fall to his knees and stood on either side of him, panting for breath. *Oh, Lord*, Bertwoin thought, no longer distracted by his thoughts, *we're only halfway*. How would he ever finish this trek?

"We must get on," the monk in charge insisted. "The bishop waits for him."

"*We're* doing the hauling work, monk, not you," grumbled Scar-eye.

"The abbot will hear of your disobedience."

The guards ignored the monks and squatted with Bertwoin between them.

Their little band had, of course, attracted everyone's notice. The high-born, other monks, and merchants crossing the Aude, some riding horses, smiled to praise the brothers who had captured this criminal.

Farmers and their wives, traveling musicians, tradespeople, and servants glanced at Bertwoin with outright pity. Some stopped and stood in small, whispering groups. The Church's tithes on lambs and its fees for services made it no friends among those who worked. Many people hated the pompous clerics who lived off their toil.

The monks, at least, did their own manual labor and helped the poor, but their abbey was wealthy, and the rules of their order were less closely followed now than in earlier years. Most of the brothers were noble-born and expected indulgence.

The monks on the bridge relaxed in a small cluster and pretended to be completely absorbed in a discussion of Brother Gregorius's latest vision. But they were as alert as a cat pretending not to notice a mouse. They were very aware of their audience and had fallen into the sin of pride.

Tisbe, the brew mistress, strode toward Bertwoin in a long, blue tunic with her abundant hair stuffed under a hemp coif. She carried a dripping cloth she had dipped in the Aude.

The lead monk stepped forward with a contemptuous

smile and blocked her way. "Get on with your business, woman, or you'll regret it."

"Someone needs to tend to him."

The brother flicked his fingers. "Get away with you."

She tossed the wet cloth past the righteous brother onto Bertwoin's knee. Neither guard moved. Bertwoin grabbed it and wiped his face with it just before a brother snatched it out of his hand. Tisbe eyed Bertwoin with defiant sympathy.

Bertwoin took solace in the fact that she didn't believe he had drowned Emeline. He vowed to pay back her simple kindness with plowing.

The lead monk said, "It's time to go." He warned the two squatting laymen, "The abbot will hear of your weakness. Unless he decides to be charitable, neither of you will work for us again."

Scar-eye stood up and said, "Those are welcome words to me, you sanctimonious ass. Remember," he added with a spiteful smile, "you were born a bastard."

The arrogant brother glared at him, his face a mask of hatred. "Begone, cur."

The guard shoved his way through the grouped brothers instead of going around them and swaggered away. The other guard hesitated, then grabbed Bertwoin's left arm and hoisted him to standing. The lead monk motioned for a plump, sturdy brother to grab Bertwoin's other arm.

They trudged toward the bishop's palace in St. Vincent. To distract his attention away from his misery, Bertwoin again concentrated on his thoughts.

Even if he didn't hang for killing Emeline, the abbot meant to punish him for the crime of desecration, or whatever he called the sin in Latin. At the very least, Abbot Jehan would see he was publicly whipped for trespassing.

Somehow, with tiny shuffling steps and the help of the sweating pear-shaped guard and sturdy monk, Bertwoin hiked the rest of the way to St. Vincent. People stood back against the walls of wattle-and-daub houses and shops to watch them pass. The lead monk strutted in front of their group, proud as a crusader entering a conquered town.

By noon, most folks in Carcassonne and the towns below it would know that the monks had captured him. His *maman* and father would hear of it and know to bring him food. Had he disgraced their *ostal's* spirit and damned its luck?

The *bayle* would raise his tankard and toast these monks. They had relieved him of having to hunt, find, and arrest Clanoud's eldest son.

Fractious Tolarto appeared and hurried toward them, grinning like a malicious imp. "Not so high and mighty now, are you? I hope they rip out your fingernails and crack your bones, pig shit. I'll dance when I see you choking and kicking at the end of a rope."

The lead monk looked back over his shoulder. "Hold your tongue, churl, and get on about your business."

Ignoring the brother, Tolarto continued to prance along beside them. "With my own eyes, I saw him with Emeline. He murdered her, Agbart's innocent girl. He's a butt crack who thinks he's better than others. He thinks it sport to insult people in the market."

"Why are *you* not arrested, pig-poacher?" Bertwoin shouted despite his headache. "You skulked in the woods where Emeline died. Why do they not question you?"

"Oh, so to save yourself you claim I was there too?"

"You said it yourself, mule's ass. How could you see me talking with Emeline if you weren't there? Did you stalk her in the woods?"

"Liar," Tolarto yelled.

He lunged for Bertwoin, trying to push past the monk holding him up. The brother shoved the muleteer away.

Off-balance, Bertwoin stumbled sideways against the

small guard, who bawled at Tolarto, "Dumb owl shit." He rushed at the muleteer with his club raised.

But by now, the lead monk and another brother had rushed forward to help the one at Bertwoin's side. They formed a black-robed wall between Tolarto and their prisoner.

"Get away, peasant, or I will have you arrested," the lead monk yelled up into Tolarto's face.

"Arrest him now," Bertwoin shouted. "He was there. I saw him run into the woods that day."

"Liar," Tolarto yelled. He stood at bay, faced by three monks with his back against the whitewashed wall of a house.

"I'll let the abbot know of you, peasant," the lead monk barked at Tolarto. "He'll see you shamed and fined for this."

"Go to Hell, priest's wife," Tolarto snarled.

"I'll not let you harm him, mule-packer," a man shouted.

Everyone, including Tolarto, turned toward the voice.

Bertwoin blinked and focused his bleary sight on Villenc, the relentless brother of Sebastian who had expected to marry Emeline.

The stonebreaker swaggered toward Tolarto, and the monks backed away. "The plowman did our house a favor if he killed that heretical little bitch."

"I never harmed her," Bertwoin said.

Villenc rubbed a calloused hand over his bald scalp, nodded, and admitted, "You don't seem the type. But if you *are* innocent, then this toad turd here has no reason to torment you."

Tolarto said nothing. Stocky Villenc, like Clanoud, was stronger than any blacksmith and not someone you insulted within his hearing.

The brothers and layman guard again formed a group around Bertwoin and began marching him up the crowded street. Tolarto leaned sullenly against the daub wall, his way still blocked by the hostile stonebreaker.

Bertwoin hoped they reached the fortress soon. His strength was leaking away like wine from a punctured leather bag. He longed only for the comfort of a dark dungeon cell where he could lay his forehead against a cool, stone floor.

They arrived at the bishop's fortress—a four-story palace adorned with towers, slanted slate roofs, and a formal garden that would do honor to the King of Aragon. Under it was their destination, a dungeon with rats, torturers, confessors, and, of course, criminals...and sometimes victims like himself who were treated as criminals.

A gatekeeper wearing green livery resembling a silk suit on a noblewoman's monkey waved them through the imposing entrance.

The pear-shaped guard shoved him two faltering steps along the inside of the outer brick wall and muttered, "We wait here."

Bertwoin squatted and leaned back against the rough bricks. His eyelids were warm with fatigue. The ale-stinking guard grunted into a squat beside him.

The haughty lead monk swaggered across an open area and skipped up the wide marble steps of the proud entrance. A doorman, also in monkey livery, stopped him before letting him enter.

After some time, the lead monk strode back out onto the porch, proud as a new father, and waved to one side of the residence.

The pear-shaped guard rose and said to Bertwoin, "Let's go."

Bertwoin walked toward the side of the palace the monk had indicated, trying to keep his head high and back straight, but it taxed his strength to lurch one slow step forward at a time. It was easier to slump.

Around the front corner, Bertwoin came to a dozen steps leading to a solid oak door below ground level. Unsure of his balance, Bertwoin hesitated. Each stone step was slick with age and worn down in the middle. The pear-shaped guard grabbed the back of his woolen tunic to keep him from falling and held him up as they descended.

The guard opened the door and said, "Your new home."

Bertwoin gulped a last breath of fresh air before the man prodded him into a dark corridor with the end of his cudgel.

A fat warder with four large keys on his belt slumped on a high stool, sleeping with his back propped in a corner and his chin on his chest. Bertwoin's guard honked like a goose.

The sluggish warder slowly opened his eyes. "So, what have you brought me today, Luc?"

The layman guard's laugh echoed faintly in the dim corridor. "One who doesn't hesitate to give a monk a hard smack on the snout."

Surprised, Bertwoin raised his drooping head. Instead of announcing him as a foul murderer, Luc had praised him for hitting a monk.

The warder chuckled. "So this is the one." He tapped his forehead, then pointed at Bertwoin's forehead. "I share your opinion of those who pray, though I'd sooner smack a priest than a monk."

"You're a shepherd then?" Bertwoin asked.

Luc asked, "Aren't we all?"

"Yes," the warder said, "and the Church bleeds us weak with its tithes and taxes and duties." He pointed at the low ceiling, indicating the palace above them. "Someone has to pay so the bishop can eat duck breast and ride a fine stallion."

Luc said to Bertwoin, "May the abbot only fine you or whip you and not see fit to break your knuckles, plowman. May you have God's luck." He saluted the warder and left them.

The warder rose from his stool as if it were a chore he dreaded. "Let me show you to your bedroom, monk-smacker."

"That will be to your profit," Bertwoin said to let the warder know he would receive something in return for taking good care of him.

"Well, cause me no trouble, and you'll receive none from me," the warder said, accepting his offer. "Brothers of the flocks should help each other when they can. Turn around so I can untie your hands."

Bertwoin sighed when the rope came loose, though blood tingled painfully into his white fingers.

His room had once been more than just a dungeon cell. Its oak door, which looked sturdy enough to withstand a battering ram, hinted at palatial splendor. Above it, a religious coat of arms carved in blue and white marble showed a haloed female saint. She held a cross and chalice with a lamb on either side of her.

Bertwoin made the sign of the cross before passing under her into his cell. He stopped a moment to pray silently for her to help the alchemist prove him innocent.

The warder locked the door behind him and shuffled away.

The stone floor of the narrow room was bare except for his bed—a mound of unbound straw piled along one wall. A stool sat in one corner. In another corner was an empty bucket for his business. The window was small and barred, its view that of a corner tower set in the outer wall.

Bertwoin grunted down onto his straw bed, which smelled fresh. The warder had given him a good room. He closed his raw eyes, let his heavy head rest on the sweet-scented straw, and sighed.

The master alchemist now had to find Roqua and search for clues without him.

CHAPTER XIV.

B ertwoin woke when the warder shoved a clanging key into the lock on his cell door and creaked it open. A bony hand reached out and dropped a silver coin on the smiling warder's palm.

Then the alchemist stepped around the oak door and ducked into the cell. What better friend did Bertwoin have than this man, who was almost a stranger to him? He started to rise, but the master patted the air for him to stay on his straw bed.

After the warder locked the door, the alchemist listened a moment, his expression grim in the stark, white light coming through the cell's window. He pulled the stool out of its corner and sat on it, leaning forward with his elbows on his bony knees.

"Has Brother Theodoric come to see about your head?"

"No, master, not yet," Bertwoin shrugged. "It's no more than a dull ache. Less of a problem than having my neck snapped for murder."

"We must take care that your neck suffers no injury." The

alchemist made a point of surveying the cell. "Your prison is snug and fairly clean."

Bertwoin lay on his side with his cheek resting on his palm, his bent elbow in the straw. He twirled his free hand. "May I offer you a glass of Bordeaux wine? You have the choice of red or white."

"Ah, the red king or white queen. A difficult choice." The alchemist cocked his head and stared up at the brick ceiling as if deciding which wine to choose.

Men's voices sounded in the passageway outside the cell's door.

"Red king, white queen?" Bertwoin asked.

"They're symbols. They can mean different things to different alchemists, but normally, the red man or red king is iron. The white woman or white queen is antimony."

Again the key rattled in the lock, the door opened, and the *bayle* barged into the room. The warder didn't lock the door after he closed it.

As usual, the ex-crusader wore his leather tunic with the red cross on it and a silk hat held in place by a red ribbon. He smiled down at Bertwoin and rubbed his hands together as if preparing to perform a task he relished. "So I see the monks caught the rabbit."

The man's smug satisfaction would irritate an angel. "Agbart hasn't come to rescue me yet."

The lawman grinned. "He did do that when I came for you, didn't he? Sometimes what we do brings us the opposite of what-"

"This rabbit is more victim than villain," the master said.

The *bayle* leaned back against a wall. "So you say. Anyway, it's up to my betters to judge him, not me. My duty was only to catch him."

Bertwoin stifled an urge to remind the lawman that he hadn't done so. He also didn't remind him of the fact that he was the one who had decided only this rabbit needed catching, none of the others.

"Our plowman here," the alchemist continued, "doesn't wear sandals, something the murderer did."

"To prove such a thing would need more magic than you have, old man. By the by, Sir Jean-Luc is not pleased with you. You gave sanctuary to a criminal I was hunting, a charge the bishop is sure to mention to the *visconte*."

"I had hoped that my doing so would turn you toward finding the real killer instead of just seeking the easiest answer. The *visconte* will understand that."

The *bayle* dismissed this with a downward slap. "I usually find that the simplest answer is the right one."

"And I simply wanted you to find the true killer before he killed again."

"Been looking into the future, have you?"

"No. I rely on experience. Like you, I have seen a multitude of criminals. But experience is only profitable for those who are willing to learn from it. Remember, I have already solved three murders for the *visconte*." He shrugged. "And as for our young plowman here, you will have to argue against the fact that he was with me when the same murderer killed Roqua."

The *bayle* lurched away from the wall. "Roqua? You know this for certain?"

"I found her." The alchemist closed his eyes. "Or what was left of her."

"Oh," Bertwoin said. He put his forehead in his hand and moaned.

"And only you knew where to find her," the *bayle* said.

The master leaned back in the cell's corner and stretched out his long legs. "No magic necessary. She was missing, and I *reasoned* that the murderer might repeat the method of his first crime. I searched near the area where Janus had found poor Emeline."

As the lawman should have done, Bertwoin thought.

"And the plowman here," the *bayle* nodded at Bertwoin, "was with you when Roqua went missing? All of the time?"

"He was in my house."

"And you were there the entire time."

"I was in Béziers, but he would have an easier time slipping away from me than he would from Flowia."

"And she would never lie for him?"

"She would not lie to me."

The lawman bit his lower lip as he considered this. "Ah, could be. In my belly, I never really believed Bertwoin here killed the woodcutter's daughter, but it was my duty to arrest him and make certain he hadn't. Brother Nigellus gave telling evidence against him. I was looking at others too."

The alchemist raised an eyebrow but said nothing.

Bertwoin kept his face friendly. The *bayle* was now going to pretend he had never doubted his innocence and had only been doing his duty. But he had allowed Brother Nigellus to distract him and make him pursue an innocent plowman. He had ignored other suspects, including Brother Nigellus himself. He had given the murderer time to kill again.

The *bayle* squinted at the alchemist. "So you found Roqua and told no one of this?"

The master glanced at the ceiling as if asking God to give him patience. "Why do you assume that?"

"*I* knew nothing of it."

"If I had told you, you might have named me guilty and arrested me. That would be the simplest answer."

"And still is."

"I told Prior Simon where to find Roqua's remains."

The *bayle* nodded. "He's the only one at the abbey who'll respect the corpse of a female heretic enough to carry it home. Well, I guess I should visit Gertrude's and take a look at Roqua's body."

He strutted to the door and faced Bertwoin. "You're still a suspect until the seneschal tells me otherwise. You resisted my arrest. You'll also answer to the abbot, even if someone else confesses to the killing of Emeline. The rabbit tweaked his nose, and the abbot intends to skin it."

"I didn't resist your arrest. The woodcutter did it for me. And he attacked you. Yet he still walks free."

The *bayle* scowled at the master. "And you, old rooster, will answer for hiding an accused man from the *visconte* and the Church."

After the lawman left them, Bertwoin asked the alchemist, "So you found Roqua in the pit in the linden grove?"

The master bowed his head and massaged his brow with his fingertips. "Yes, the killer hadn't bothered to remove her corpse." He nodded at the door. "Our *bayle* wasn't curious enough to ask me where I found Roqua's body. He won't know where to look when another young woman goes missing."

Bertwoin understood the importance of the master saying "when" instead of "if." He took a deep breath and let it out slowly. "So it was worse than last time?"

"Very much so. Her corpse is nothing but strips of charred flesh holding together a skeleton. Still, I was able to determine that her tongue had been cut in two."

Bertwoin growled, "And no one heard or saw anything?"

The master shook his head. "Not that I know of. I did find a burned remnant of cloth stuck to Roqua's teeth. So he muffled her screams."

The alchemist's laugh was bitter. "I once heard a Good Woman preach that when a martyr is burned at the stake, God steals away the pain so he or she feels only joy. This

Good Woman had never witnessed a burning. If the killer had not gagged Roqua, her screams would have woken even the deaf in Carcassonne."

His face tight, the old man stared straight ahead a moment, his sight turned inward. Then he said, "I found a footprint in the mud. That of a sandal, not a clog or a naked foot."

"A religieux?"

The master hummed agreement. "Probably. I had guessed as much. But we can't take that as a certain truth. Others besides monks and clerics wear sandals." He glanced at those on his own feet.

Bertwoin sat up and waited two breaths for the jab of pain in his head to fade away.

The alchemist frowned at him. "It distressed Flowia that you took such a blow to your head. The ache does not seem to be as dull as you claim it is."

Bertwoin waved away the seriousness of his headache. "Now both of Clanoud's sons know the feel of a knock on the head. It's a good thing our pates are thicker than a ram's skull. At least now that the *bayle* knows the killer wore sandals, he knows to search for the murderer among men of prayer, either a village priest or a wandering brother. And Abbot Jehan must look at his own flock. That should turn his mind away from me."

"I think you misjudge our proud abbot. No shame must ever strike his abbey, not while he has charge of it. He's as ambitious as a cardinal."

"But he can't let his prior or whoever the murderer is just run around and kill innocent young women," Bertwoin said, his voice loud with outrage. "Roqua was maybe eighteen, Emeline only thirteen or fourteen. What sins could they have committed that warranted their deaths?"

The master rubbed his forehead. "Only one sin is needed.

Both of these young women sympathized with the Good Folk. The Church judges those who dare to call themselves True Christians as heretics. By the way, unlike you, plowman, I doubt Prior Simon's guilt. At first, I told him only that I had found Roqua and asked him to retrieve her body. I didn't say where it lay. It was a crude trap, of course, and the prior doesn't lack brains, but he did avoid my ruse by asking me where to find her corpse."

"But it's still possible he *is* this sick killer."

The master nodded. "I also asked Prior Simon if any brothers missed their night prayers. He said only those who Brother Theodoric had excused for ill health. So we may need to look outside of the abbey for our murderer. A rabid priest would do very well."

"None of the local ones are the killing type. But the bishop has men under him who are religious maniacs."

The alchemist rubbed his bony hands together. "Ah well, right now, it is you I have the most concern for."

"I'll survive. The abbot cares more about my sneaking into his abbey and punching one of his monks than he does about these murders." Bertwoin twirled a hand to indicate his cell. "As for this, it's no worse than sleeping in our barn. And here I don't even have to work. The warder is kind enough, and look, I even receive distinguished visitors."

The alchemist raised a bony forefinger. "Oh, I forgot. I brought you some hard cheese and bread." He pulled these out of his leather bag. "I had an apple, but the warder took it when he searched my pouch."

He raised a hand to stop Bertwoin from rising and brought the food to his bed. Then he sat back down on the stool.

"But you may yet take the blame for these foul murders. The abbot may decide to sacrifice a pawn."

"Me? Why?"

"Think, plowman. The abbot can't accept having a monk of his flock accused of murdering young women, even if they are heretics. Not if he hopes to wield more power someday. And if it is one of the bishop's men, the abbot will see to it that he does the bishop the favor of keeping the problem hidden. He will say God's judgment came down on them. He might find it convenient to say you were God's means of punishing them."

"But the murderer killed Roqua while I was in your house."

"He will choose to believe Flowia and I are lying to protect you or that you sneaked away for a few hours."

"What if the killer strikes again while I am in the bishop's dungeon?"

"What if he doesn't?" the alchemist asked. "He might think it a fine joke to wait until you are hanged for his murders before he strikes down another young maiden. This would show the people how incompetent the authorities are."

"Do you think it possible he will never kill again?"

"No, I do not. Killing brings him too much joy. But he can murder you without raising his hand. He only has to wait until you dangle from the Gallows Oak before he strikes again."

The alchemist moistened his thin lips with the tip of his tongue. "If the abbot does find this wolf among his sheep, he will send him away so he doesn't kill *here* again. If the murderer continues to find victims elsewhere, what is that to Abbot Jehan? And the murderer, if caught elsewhere, might even remove some other abbot, maybe one of Jehan's rivals, from competition for higher office."

"But that's...that's...." Bertwoin slapped the straw in anger.

"Monstrous and self-serving?"

"Do you think anyone will ever find this killer?"

"Ah well, the abbot may already know who it is, especially

if it's one of his flock. And the bishop too will not want a foul murderer found among the Church officials in his diocese. So they will wring a confession from you, plowman, one that even the *visconte* must accept."

Bertwoin slapped his straw bed again. "They'll not get one from me."

"Bertwoin, you will confess. You will plead for a shameful hanging if it will stop the torturers from dislocating your joints and breaking your bones. You will accept the yoke over your neck for these crimes." The master shrugged. "This is only my supposition, of course, but I think it likely."

"So what can I do?"

"I think the answer lies in transmutation."

"What?"

The alchemist jerked his chin toward the closed door, letting him know the warder probably had his ear against it. Bertwoin realized the master wanted to be overheard. He wanted it known that he had found a sandal print where Roqua had died. He wanted the warder to spread the rumor that the killer might be a religieux. But now he wanted to hide the meaning of his words. The problem was that like his jailer, Bertwoin didn't know what transmutation meant.

The master smiled at his apparent confusion. "Isak told me today that his knuckles throbbed with pain. That usually means it will rain tonight." Pleased, the alchemist slapped his thin thigh. "Yes, everyone will sleep well tonight. Even animals will keep to their burrows and be less alert."

"Ah," Bertwoin said. Though he still had no idea what was wanted of him, he now knew something important would take place this very night, and rain might be needed to make it happen.

The alchemist raised his voice even louder. "I will send Flowia to tend to your head. Also, I think it appropriate that a few monks visit you and pray for your deliverance."

"Monks? Who would-"

The master patted the air to silence him.

"Flowia insists on coming to you with her bag of cures and some food. Monks will accompany her. She should not walk alone, especially at night, until this monster is caught."

Still not understanding what this was all about, Bertwoin said, "Of course. I still have a few friends among the monks at the abbey."

"They will be interested in your transmutation."

CHAPTER XV.

Sunset had given the light coming through the cell's tiny window a golden glow when Bertwoin heard Flowia's soft voice in the corridor outside his door, "We've come to minister to your new prisoner."

The jovial warder laughed. "I hope that if I'm ever on the other side of that door, four friends will come to visit me." There was a pause, then, "You're too kind, maiden."

So the warder had earned at least two of the alchemist's coins today, true pieces that wouldn't flake off silver coatings and reveal lead underneath. Bertwoin sighed. This meant he had to earn deniers to repay the master.

The door swung open, and the warder said to Bertwoin, "Visitors."

Flowia stepped into the doorway. The descending sunlight fell straight as an arrow's flight across her face, which looked concerned yet determined. Three monks with their cowls pulled low over their heads followed her into his cell, their arms crossed over their bellies, their hands inside the wide woolen sleeves of their black habits.

Bertwoin rose with a grunt. Pain pulsed through his

skull. He frowned at the young monks who continued to stare humbly at the brick floor. One he recognized as a farmer. Another worked as a muleteer for Isak, the cloth merchant.

They all waited quietly for the warder to shut the oak door and leave. As with the *bayle*, he didn't bother to relock it. The muleteer placed his ear against the thick door to learn whether the warder had moved back down the corridor. He placed a forefinger over his lips to let them know the guard had stayed to listen at the door.

"You are well?" Flowia asked Bertwoin.

He shrugged. "My eyesight is clearing, and my head is not broken, but I don't feel like dancing."

The third fake brother, a woodworker, barked laughter. "Your head is made of ash and is a match for any cudgel."

Everyone, even Bertwoin, chuckled. "Well, brother," he said, "I'll make sure to keep it away from you so you cannot carve a bowl for some monk's pottage out of it."

"Making a bowl would not test my skill," the woodworker told him. "It already has the emptiness of one. I need only cut your skull in half to make two bowls."

Flowia lifted the flap of her leather pouch and pulled out a small loaf of bread, which she handed to Bertwoin.

"Thank you." He devoured it in four bites.

When he eyed her pouch, she shook her head. "It's all I brought this time, but I will soon fetch you something to drink."

He spread his hands in gratitude. "You're an angel walking the Earth."

"Let us see, then, if I can redeem your soul."

"You mean transmutation?"

Flowia smiled sweetly. She nodded at the farmer monk, who to Bertwoin's surprised pulled up the hem of his habit and unwound a cowled robe wrapped around his waist.

Flowia glided closer to Bertwoin and whispered, "Now we will wait until the night guard comes to replace this warder."

She crossed the cell to the lone stool in a corner and sat while the farmer and woodworker dropped onto his bed. Bertwoin joined them. The muleteer continued to lean against the heavy door and listen for the guard.

The woodworker asked, "Shall we pray?" When no one answered, he shrugged at their lack of humor.

Bertwoin watched dying sunlight rise from the muleteer's shoulder to his cowl, creep up the brick wall over the oak door, then sneak across the ceiling before fading to a twilight glow.

The muleteer became alert and cleared his throat for their attention. "The night warder has come."

They heard the men joking and laughing, then the corridor went quiet.

"Did he tell the number of monks?" Flowia asked.

The muleteer shook his head. "Not that I heard. They just laughed and said the plowman must be a great sinner if it takes so many brothers to pray for his soul." His expression turned grave. "The night man also said the plowman's soul was sure to leave his body soon."

Flowia rose gracefully. "Well, I think his soul is beyond redemption. So instead, let's turn our efforts to saving his neck." She jerked her chin at Bertwoin. "Take off your tunic and put on the extra robe." She glanced at his bare feet and pulled a pair of sandals out of her large leather pouch.

Bertwoin stood up and blinked to clear away a moment of dizziness. He could only hope that once they sneaked out of this dungeon cell, no one would chase them. A crippled beggar on two crutches could outrun him.

The farmer snickered as he watched Bertwoin pull the monk's robe down over his linen undergarment and said, "Now we have a sheep in wolf's clothing."

Flowia tossed the sandals onto the dusty bricks at Bertwoin's feet. "These are the biggest we could find." She picked up his woolen tunic and stuffed it into her pouch.

He warned her, "The night warder might search your pouch."

"Why? Will he think I stole straw from your bed?" She made a point of inspecting his cell. "Oh, the stool. I might steal a stool from the bishop's dungeon. It would be useful at home."

Bertwoin remembered that the warder had inspected the master's pouch and asked Flowia, "How is it that the day man didn't search your bag when you came in?"

The farmer's face turned impish with glee. "She distracted him with a coin at just the right moment. Then she strutted past him like a duchess. It was expertly done."

Smiling, she nodded to thank him for his compliment. Bertwoin hoped the farmer didn't intend to court her. Onfroi was enough competition.

The woodworker laughed and clapped him on the back, making him wince. "Why not join us, Brother Wooden Head?"

"Raise your cowl," Flowia told Bertwoin.

Even in the growing dark, he could see that Flowia was tight-lipped. Then she shook her head as if shaking away her doubts and swaggered to the door. She hesitated, took a deep breath, then jerked it open.

Bertwoin saw they were in luck. The new warder hadn't yet lit a candle. The tallow tapers probably came at his own expense, and he wanted to make sure that one lasted him the entire night. So the dusky corridor's darkness would blur their faces.

Flowia stepped into the passageway and strode toward the warder as he slid off his high stool. Bertwoin realized she wanted to keep the man where he was, away from the cell, so he couldn't peer inside and see that now no prisoner stood among the monks. She held up a coin, its silver barely noticeable in the shadows, and the warder's eyes focused on her bribe instead of them.

Flowia handed the warder the denier and said, "I mean to return alone with ale for the plowman. Should I bring you some too?"

He licked his meaty lips. "That would be kind, maiden. The air down here dries out a man's throat."

The farmer adjusted his cowl, stepped to the cell's doorway, and glanced back. He motioned for Bertwoin to follow the muleteer.

The woodworker went last. Before he closed the cell's door, he called out, "We'll return tomorrow," as if Bertwoin still occupied the empty room.

The farmer and muleteer eased humbly past Flowia as she told the warder, "It may be some time before I return."

"I have all night, maiden," the warder said and grinned.

Bertwoin shuffled past him, his face averted and eyes staring at the worn bricks below his scuffling sandals. The farmer sauntered down the passageway, leading them. Bertwoin's legs trembled with pent-up energy. Why was this corridor so damnably long? Finally, the farmer squeaked open the outer door.

After they had climbed the slick steps, they stopped in the open air of the palace grounds and waited for Flowia. Bertwoin breathed deeply. He smiled up at the darkening night sky decorated with new stars and rolled his neck to rid it of kinks.

There would be no rain this night. Isak's bones had misled him. Still, the master had performed his transmutation, turning a plowman into a monk and a prisoner into a free man.

Flowia came bustling out. "Go now. I will follow you in a moment."

"Alone?" Bertwoin asked in surprise.

"The gate guards will have changed. The new ones might wonder why monks have me in tow and watch us more closely. Walking alone, I will draw attention away from you."

The farmer nodded and led the fake brothers around the corner to the entrance. They shuffled humbly through the open gate without the guards bothering to acknowledge them. Monks passing in and out of the compound at all hours was a common sight.

When they reached the wooden bridge over the Aude, they stopped to wait for Flowia. She hurried up to them and thanked them, handing each of the three fake monks a coin. Bertwoin held out his hand for one. Flowia laughed and slapped it aside.

"You already owe the master six deniers for this escape, plowman," she said. "Do you wish to make it seven?"

"We will leave you now, brother," the smiling muleteer told Bertwoin. "If caught in these black robes, we'll be whipped."

The farmer spread his arms to display his habit and looked down its front. "A shame to take them off, though. I'm told maidens like a man in a black habit." He glanced at Flowia to see if this were true.

Her lips twisted into a wry smile. "Your experience with maidens seems limited. It's how the man fills out the robe that attracts the maiden, not the woolen cloth on his back."

Bertwoin wondered if Brother Nigellus believed his dark habit made him attractive to young women.

"Then I don't need the robe," the farmer said. He held up his coin. "Tisbe's tavern will not be empty of me tonight."

"The master waits for you at his house, Brother Wooden Head," the woodworker told Bertwoin. "Give him our greetings and our thanks for hiring us. Let's hope the warder still waits for Flowia to bring him ale and hasn't yet checked on his prisoner."

"Bless you," Bertwoin told the men. "I'll not forget this."

"Neither shall I," gloated the muleteer. "Someday, when I have a wife and children, I'll tell them of this trick."

The delighted young men hurried away and faded into the new night.

CHAPTER XVI

The alchemist was sitting alone, playing chess by candlelight on his kitchen table when they pranced into the front room, flush with success.

"Who's winning?" Bertwoin crowed.

"I am," the master said, amused by his capering.

"Who's losing?"

"I am doing that too."

The master poured red ale into two clay mugs and waved for them to join him. "So it went well, I see." His expression was grave, and his brow furrowed despite their obvious success.

"It went well for me," Bertwoin agreed as he sat down. Earnest with gratitude, he turned to Flowia, who was putting three sticks on the dying hearth fire. "I only hope you don't suffer for this. You couldn't hide your face under a cowl like the others. The warder will name you."

She came over to join them and flicked a louse off the table. "I knew the risk."

The master moved a tall chess piece and turned his stern gaze on Bertwoin. "When the abbot learns that you escaped and that Flowia helped you, he'll order his monks to search our *ostal*. I must get word to the carter tonight that when he leaves tomorrow morning, he is to take you to where our sheep are pastured."

Bertwoin doubted he could hike that far. Just trekking from the bishop's palace to this house had turned his muscles into oozing mud. "The clout to my head has made me too weak to walk that far. Besides, they'll now come for Flowia as well."

The alchemist hummed agreement. "I know, but she was leaving anyway. She has a more compelling reason to hide." He glared at her.

"I'm sorry," she said. "I just thought we should lure this murderer out of his hole."

"What?" Bertwoin asked in alarm.

"Yes," the old man said, "she reasoned that the killer is a religieux who seeks out young, female heretics. Since the killer might consider her also heretical, she used this to have Roqua bait a trap for her."

"What?" Bertwoin said again.

The master scowled at the tall chess piece he had moved and slid it back to where it had been. He smiled at Flowia. "Ah well, it is time for me to stretch my neck, flap my wings, and forgive your mistake."

He rubbed his forehead. "I have reconsidered our decision to hide you at my sister's *ostal*. You won't be completely safe there. Bertwoin, of course, can still flee to the mountains, but living among outlaw shepherds is no place for a young woman, even a feisty one."

"I have cousins a day's travel from here," Bertwoin said. "That might be far enough away to be out from under the bishop's nose."

The alchemist tapped his finger on the table. "We need to

hide her somewhere farther beyond the reach of the bishop and the *bayle*."

Frowning, Flowia put her hands on her hips. "When both of you decide how to dispose of me, do inform me."

The alchemist pretended to be shocked. "You mean you wish to have a say in where you hide?"

Bertwoin took a sip of ale and straightened his tired back. "If I'm in Catalonia, I can't help you find the murderer. And if Flowia is far away, neither can she. I know a secret place where the monks, the bishop, the *bayle*, and Agbart will never think to look for us. We can outfox them. I'm thinking of hiding in—"

The goldsmith raised a thin hand. "If I knew, it would only cause me to worry. And if I don't know, even torture can't draw the answer from me." He laughed at Bertwoin's look of alarm. "It won't come to that. Though if it ever did and I was out of my mind with pain, I couldn't guarantee I wouldn't tell them where you were hiding. As I said, secrets have a way of announcing themselves."

"Roqua never would have told on Bertwoin," Flowia protested, "even if she saw him in the workshop that day."

"Not knowingly," the master said. "But Roqua was Roqua. She was never one to keep silent about what she knew. If she whispered her bit of gossip to one of the Good Folk, someone she trusted, and they told another, then a Church spy might have learned where he hid."

They sat a moment in silence, each one considering whether Roqua had seen Bertwoin and told someone. Then the alchemist said, "Whether you travel alone or not, plowman, you had best eat your fill before you leave."

Flowia got up and began laying food on the table. "I hope this place you've chosen is safe."

Bertwoin shrugged. "I've hidden there before without being found."

The master tapped Bertwoin's forearm. "Flowia didn't expect to hide with you, but if she agrees to do so, I will feel easier."

Bertwoin grinned at the prospect. "Why wouldn't she? With her brains and my brawn, we're a match for the Pope himself."

The goldsmith shook his head in mock despair. "Two lambs planning to tie a knot in a wolf's tail." He picked up a black chess piece. "This piece is called a bishop. Our *visconte* will ask our bishop often, especially in public, if you have been caught yet. Thus will he remind everyone who hears him that you escaped from the bishop's mighty fortress on the Aude and outwitted the churchman."

"Me? It was you and Flowia who tricked him."

"Ah well, we *can* take some credit for that." The alchemist raised his hooked nose and made a point of sniffing the air. "Will these hounds in black habits come for you soon, or will they not know the rabbit escaped its cage until morning? I think the night warder, even if he discovers you gone, will be loath to report that he has lost a prisoner. Better to say nothing and let the day warder find himself with an empty cell. The bishop will want to blame your escape on one of his jailors. By punishing him, he will let everyone know you outsmarted his warder, not him."

Bertwoin sighed. "Too bad. The warder was friendly to me."

Flowia went into one of the bedrooms and returned with two leather pouches. So she had decided to go with him after all. She began filling the pouches with hard cheese, smoked meat, and barley bread.

"I will stay here to welcome the abbey's men," the master said, "and try to lessen the damage they do to our home while they search it. Then I must be away for two or three days."

Flowia asked, "You are leaving?"

"I know a nobleman not far from here who practices our arts. He has excellent equipment. I think together we may determine if the strand I found under Emeline's fingernails comes from an animal or a plant. I want to know if it is wool or hemp or linen."

He clapped his bony hands. "But my mind won't be at ease until both of you are away." He smiled at Flowia. "You did well this night, daughter."

She ducked her head shyly. Watching her, Bertwoin again felt uplifted with gratitude. She had put herself at risk for him and was now willing to trust him enough to hide with him in his secret place.

When they were ready to leave, the master raised a hand over their heads. "Take care, lambs. May angels spread their wings over you and protect you."

Flowia kissed his bearded cheek. The alchemist nodded goodbye to Bertwoin. "If it is safe, come see me in a few days. Until then, remember it is often wise to follow this one's direction." He lifted his chin to indicate Flowia.

Bertwoin pulled the cowl of his black monk's robe over his head and went out into the warm night to give Flowia a moment alone with the master.

He took a deep breath and whispered, "Please let me be right about our hiding place."

CHAPTER XVII

T hey hiked in silence under a radiant moon. Bertwoin heard Flowia sob but didn't look at her so as not to intrude into her misery. Like him, she was now a fugitive who ran from one peril to another.

Then Flowia stopped, frowning. "We're walking toward the bishop's palace when we should be fleeing in the opposite direction."

"I know what I'm doing."

"They won't need to search for us if you take us back to the dungeon." She stopped, but he kept walking. After a moment, she began following him again. He slowed to let her catch up.

"I was going to take refuge with Gertrude," she told him.

"The monks and clerics will either watch or search all of the heretic houses. They would welcome finding you there. It would give them an excuse to punish a Good Woman. Besides, someone bringing her food might see you, as Roqua saw me in the workshop."

"Her visitors lock their secrets inside their breasts and hide what they know. They would never tell on me."

"But they would talk among themselves, as the master said. And the Church has ears pressed against every shutter and eyes watching every door."

"The master will turn you over to the abbot himself," she warned, "and see you whipped if you let the monks catch us."

"*I* will suffer the most if they catch us."

"You think that convinces me?"

Flowia stayed quiet as she followed him along the bank of the river. When they reached the abbey, he eased open a small door in the church's back wall and peeked inside. Only a single lit candle near the front doors relieved the tomblike darkness. He crept into the hushed stillness.

She didn't follow him. "You're going to claim sanctuary?"

He reminded himself that this had to be difficult for her. "No," he whispered. "I know of a secret attic in one of the storage buildings. Some of the monks don't even know of it."

"An attic?" Flowia glanced behind her at the dark woods as if she might dart into them.

"Yes, one with three rooms and a trapdoor, the only way in or out."

He listened a moment to make sure no monk lay praying with outstretched arms on the cold, stone floor. "We can hide up there and eat our fill from the supplies stored in the building under us. No one will notice us as long as we stay quiet as worms and don't become overly gluttonous."

He didn't mention that the brothers who did know about the attic avoided it because they believed it was haunted by either the ghost of a once-rebellious monk or a perverse demon. She already had enough worries.

Flowia still didn't move. "Only one door? Even a rabbit knows to build its burrow with many exits."

"I was once trapped inside the abbey for three nights and hid in that very attic." He kept his voice low and gentle. "No one found me, and I ate well. The walls have arrow slits, so we'll see any danger coming at us. And we might even hear something that will help the master find the killer."

"You still believe the prior killed them?"

He wasn't sure, but he didn't think now was the best time to argue about it. A brother coming inside the church to pray or returning from some official night business might catch them. "Let's talk about that later. Not here, not now."

She stepped inside the church and said with resignation, "Lead the way, plowman."

He figured that even if they were discovered in the abbey, they might be able to fight their way past a surprised brother or two and run to the church. If trapped there, they would simply claim the sanctuary she had mentioned and hope everyone honored their right to it.

Flowia chuckled. "I will admit, and don't let this puff you up like a strutting rooster, your choice of a hiding place is clever. It's so risky that few monks would ever dream you were silly enough to do this. Your scheme is even more daring than my plan to free you from the bishop's dungeon."

So it had been *her* plan after all. "I thought the master had fashioned it."

She nodded. "He added details."

She patted his back as he led her down a dark side aisle to the church's main doors. "Who would think to hunt for two doves in a falcon's nest?"

CHAPTER XVIII.

They hurried through the church's cool darkness to the lone candle kept lit to welcome any brother or cleric who sought the solace of night prayer. Near the front doors, Bertwoin dipped two fingers in the stoup and made the sign of the rood. He then waited and watched Flowia. She snickered, tapped a forefinger delicately on the dark puddle of holy water, and also made the sign of the cross.

"So you're not a real heretic after all," he said as if he had caught her in a lie.

"I keep my mind unveiled by prejudice."

"Do you think it possible the killer is one of the Good Folk?" he asked.

"I think Emeline and Roqua were killed because they *held* Good Folk beliefs."

Bertwoin shook his head. "Even Villenc wasn't going to kill Emeline. And most people tolerate the Good Folk."

He stared at the single taper...half its length was gone. Tallow had oozed down one side and solidified in a waxy pool at its base. Who replenished these candles and kept a flame lit inside the church all night? And how often did they come to do that?

"We must remember," he told Flowia, "never to enter or be inside this church when the lit taper nears its end."

He hoped they met no brother wandering outside his cell tonight. His head and bruised ribs still ached, and his body seemed a sluggish lump of clay. The thought of running with monks chasing him made him tired.

Bertwoin picked three tallow candles from a pile on an iron stand, stuffed two of them into the leather pouch he carried, and lit the remaining one from the taper already burning.

"We'll have to chance a lit candle if we're to have light in the attic," he said and added to reassure her, "I've sneaked into the abbey many times after dark with no mishap. But if a black-robe does spot us, I'll snuff out the flame. Hide wherever you can."

Flowia giggled, and Bertwoin reared back. Was she nervous? Or was she laughing at him because he had given her an order? Did she always have to be the one in charge?

"What?" he snapped.

Her eyes glowed with amusement. "That's every monk's dream, isn't it? To see the light?"

Relieved, he laughed and patted her shoulder. She hadn't challenged him, after all, and humor was always a welcome guest. It would honey their time together.

"Well," he said, "let's hope no monk sees our light. If one does, hide, then slip outside into the woods. I'll handle the brother. Meet me later by the *visconte's* mill."

Again she giggled, pinched her nose, and asked in a honking voice, "What does a monk's chanting sound like after you've 'handled him' by flattening his nose?"

He chuckled. Flowia did have imagination. Their time hiding together in the attic might turn out to be entertaining after all. "Think of the other brothers," he said. "How can they not laugh at his stuffy-nosed chanting? And what penance is meted out for their laughter?"

They slipped outside into the quiet courtyard. The moon silvered the trees, bushes, and the rough stones of the well in the middle.

He hurried down a long, covered gallery, his hand shielding the taper's slanted flame. Flowia shadowed along behind him. They flitted past the dark, open doorways of unoccupied rooms.

Halfway down the gallery, he turned left into a brick passageway and sped through it. They crossed the grassy area behind the inner buildings to a row of stone buildings built against the outer wall. He stopped in front of the last structure.

"Here it is," he whispered, "our secret inn run by caring brothers. We are their guests, so it will cost us nothing."

"The bishop's dungeon was also free," Flowia muttered.

Where had this sudden grumpiness come from? Was she now regretting coming with him? He hoped she wasn't going to grumble constantly and make their time together vexing. He reminded himself that he was the reason she now scurried about like a hunted mouse.

"We'll only be prisoners here during daylight," he said to lighten her mood a little. "We can sneak out at night."

She examined his face to see if he was joking, then groused, "Why would we want to roam outside in the dark like wayward souls?"

His expression turned serious. "Because the master is away right now. It's left to us to find this killer. When he comes back, he can talk to the charcoalers and Agbart. We can only talk to Gertrude. But she might know something. After all, she was Emeline's teacher and Roqua's mother."

Without warning, Flowia looked stricken, then she began to cry.

"What? Did I say something wrong?" he asked.

"I'm responsible for Roqua's death."

"How can that be?"

Flowia wiped tears off her cheeks. "I told Roqua to tell Brother Nigellus that Mary Magdalene had blessed me, that she had come to me in a vision."

"Why?"

"So the killer would notice me. Don't you see? He murdered Emeline. Why? Maybe because she was a heretic. I'm not a true *credente*, but some people call me a heretic. The murderer might think it blasphemous for me to claim I was blessed with a sacred visitation."

Bertwoin wasn't certain that falsely claiming to have a holy visitation wasn't blasphemy. "Ah, so that's why the master was vexed with you. You put yourself on the hook as bait to catch the eel." He whistled as he considered her plight. "The sick-headed killer is more dangerous than the monks and the bishop."

She nodded, still sobbing. "I didn't know the killer would punish Roqua for my blasphemy. I thought he would be frantic to find *me*."

"Do you think Brother Nigellus killed Roqua when she told him of your vision?"

"Maybe, but as the master says, how can a monk be the killer if he has to remain in the abbey almost all day and all night?"

Bertwoin glanced around at the high, moonlit buildings. "Well, they sometimes roam about inside the abbey after dark, though not often. Let's scurry to our nest and hide."

Flowia rapped on the storeroom's massive oak door as if to test its strength. "This might withstand a battering ram."

She threw her head back and judged the towering wall. "It looks more like a fortress."

"In its own way, it is. Most of the monks will take refuge in this storeroom if marauders overrun the abbey. It's well-stocked with food and drink. Those hiding inside can withstand a siege for weeks while they pray for God to send soldiers to save them."

A ponderous, wrought-iron crucifix hung on the door. Bertwoin handed Flowia their flickering taper and lifted the heavy cross off a thick hook. He picked a key as large as his hand out of a cavity in the rood's back and held it up for Flowia to see. "*Voilà*. What a battering ram cannot do, Bertwoin the resourceful plowman can."

She curtsied to show she was impressed. "An ox who uses his wiles instead of his brawn. How refreshing."

"I've smuggled supplies in here before," he told her. "Some brothers cache their private hoards among the abbey's stores."

Flowia raised her eyebrows and thought a moment before chanting, "They hide their own eggs best/by copying the cunning cuckoo/among the eggs in the abbey's nest/and so enjoy what is for them taboo."

Bertwoin laughed. "Only they don't push all of the other eggs out of this nest." He raised a cautionary finger. "So we'll need to be as wary as mice. Brothers sneak in here all the time. And not just to get what they themselves have cached. It's a game among them to find the treasures others have hidden here."

Bertwoin shoved the key into the hefty lock, clicked back the bolt, pushed the bulky door inward, and carried the cumbersome iron cross inside.

Flowia entered, raised the lit candle, and gasped. "Why did I ever pack our pouches with food?"

Dead chickens and legs of pork and mutton hung from

massive ceiling beams. Half of the room was crowded with sack after bulging sack of raw grain and flour. Barrels of ale and wine along with baby casks of spirits covered the rest of the hard-packed dirt floor.

"Yes, a mighty storeroom of plenty," Bertwoin agreed, delighted by her awe. "The monks and clerics here feed like geese being fattened for a nobleman's Christmas. Except these geese gorge during all the seasons. Praying and chanting day and night is demanding toil and calls for goodly amounts of bread, meat, cheese, and ale."

He relocked the door from the inside, tapped the cross, and said, "We have to hang this back where we found it."

Bertwoin fitted the key into its cavity on the rood, then pulled open the shutters covering the window beside the door. He threaded the heavy cross through the window's bars and was just able to reach far enough outside to hang the crucifix on the door's hook. It swung back and forth a moment, rasping a little against the wood.

Bertwoin closed the shutters and stretched like a satisfied cat. He pulled back his cowl. "No one will see our light now." Taking the taper from Flowia, he led her between barrels and bloated hemp sacks to a ladder. Its upper end led to a landing a third as large as the room on the ground floor.

"Careful," he said, pointing to a broken rung. "Must have been a well-fed brother."

The landing was loaded with stacked cheeses, bags of beans, dried beef and pork and veal, and other foodstuffs. Bertwoin picked his way through the supplies and smiled up at the plank ceiling not an arm's length above his head.

Flowia frowned. "You're saying it's there?"

Bertwoin tapped the ceiling which rang hollow. "No more solid than a minstrel's drum. A monk with too much wine in him told me about it. Pillagers may ransack this storehouse and never discover that the abbot and prior hide in secret above their heads."

Bertwoin handed Flowia their burning taper, then shoved the trapdoor aside in the dark space above them. "*Voilà*."

The smell of stale air drifted down. Bertwoin tossed his leather pouch into the upper room. He grabbed the edges of the opening and hauled himself up into the attic, huffing when pain ripped up his side.

He reached down out of the dimness and took the taper from Flowia. He dripped a tiny puddle of melted tallow on the wooden floor an arm's length from him, set the candle in it, and held it until the puddle of wax cooled enough to hold the taper upright. Then he again reached down to Flowia.

When she hesitated, he said gently, "I'll not harm you, Flowia. You have my word on it."

She stared up into the attic, now hazy with candlelight, her expression one of dismay. "It's just that there's no other exit. Once I'm inside, I'm trapped. And I know you dare not bother me. The master would make you wish-"

"The goldsmith doesn't scare me. It's just not my way to harm a maiden."

Flowia inspected his face in the flickering light. Then she gave him her leather pouch and stretched her slender hand up to him. He grasped it and stood up, letting his sturdy legs take the strain and do the grunt work of pulling her through the opening. Again, pain stitched up his side.

For half a breath, they stood face-to-face, and he smelled the rosemary wash she used on her hair. Frowning, she quickly moved away. Flowia pulled the taper loose from the floor, its flame bending sideways as she raised it aloft to inspect the attic. "So this is it?"

Bertwoin tried to see their hiding place with her virgin eyes. Dust caked the plank floor, and spider webs veiled much of the shingle roof and draped the corners. Moonlight filtered through cobwebs woven in the arrow slits of the limestone walls.

A little embarrassed by the attic's bareness, Bertwoin said, "I was probably the last person up here."

"And you stayed here three nights? That's the last time this attic was cleaned?"

"Cleaned?" He scratched his head as he scanned the walls. What good would it have done to clean an unused attic?

When she groaned in disgust but not surprise at his tolerance for spiders and filth and disorder, he gave her his best boyish look of innocence. "Well, it seemed useless to do so. Anyway," he said quickly, "let me go down and fetch us some supplies."

"Won't they miss them?"

He shook his head. "Probably not. Only brothers like Gregorius are too saintly to pilfer cheese and ale. Of course, Gregorius is always fasting anyway." Bertwoin waved at the gaping trapdoor and the supplies below them. "It's all common property, right? And those who have charge of the abbey's foodstuffs keep better count of what's owed them than what they use."

"A broom would be welcome."

"For cleaning or for riding through the air?"

"I only fly during new moons when no one can see me," she said in the low tone one used to scare children. "During full moons like tonight, I usually smear my body with a green paste made from devil's weed and dance naked with Satan at the Doorstep."

Bertwoin was too shocked to laugh.

Flowia's eyes widened, and her face twisted in mock fear. She scanned the dim attic apprehensively. "I do hope Satan doesn't miss me during the next new moon," she intoned. "There's only one way in and one way out of here when He finds me."

Disconcerted, Bertwoin frowned at her. Joking about the Devil in this fashion might bring them to His attention. Bertwoin saw that his reaction delighted her and changed the subject. "Would you like me to fetch you a tapestry too, noble maiden?"

"Yes, we'll need at least two," she said. "And bring rope or chains to hang them."

Bertwoin blinked in surprise. Her tone was serious.

Flowia pointed to hooks above the two doorways leading off their main room where curtains had once hung. "You're not alone this time, plowman. We need to hang something up for modesty."

"Ah, yes. Good idea," he said, his confidence returning. "The abbey stores most of its daily supplies and tools in the building next to this one. There's a door between the buildings, so we don't have to risk going outside for most of what we want. We need only to go out to fetch water from the well in the courtyard or fresh food and pottery from the kitchen."

He hesitated and said, "And Flowia, I don't believe you caused Roqua's death. She was already doomed. Like Emeline, she was connected to Gertrude, even more so by being her daughter. She was one of the Good Folk." His brow furrowed in thought. "And as with Emeline, Brother Nigellus made it his duty to save her soul. I wonder if he isn't the killer we seek?"

CHAPTER XIX.

S tartled by his words, Flowia stared at him with her mouth slightly open. "The two of them. Why do we assume Emeline was his first victim?"

Bertwoin didn't remember any other young women who were found burned. "You mean-"

"Yes," she hissed. "Who else did Brother Nigellus make it his business to save?"

"You mean the weaver's daughter, Brune? She did go missing, didn't she?"

"Yes. And before Emeline, he pestered Brune like a fly smelling vomit. How do we know Emeline wasn't his *second* murder? We must ask Gertrude about her."

Bertwoin eased down through the opening and dropped onto the landing. Pain speared through his head and stabbed from his injured ribs into his chest.

He was eager to share the abbey's bounty with Flowia and wanted to delight her tongue with rare tastes. Tapestries, though, had startled him. She seemed to have the trick of shocking him. He'd have to stay alert, or she would think he *was* as dumb as mutton.

Bertwoin brought her a long-handled birch broom and hauled up two straw mattresses. He found thin hemp fishing lines and cut off two lengths to stretch between the hooks above the doorways. He also cut a third length, because extra ropes and lines were always needed. He found two wide linen cloths for privacy hangings and tossed them into the attic's main room.

When he set two clunky buckets and fuzzy mullein leaves for their personal privy needs in the attic, he heard Flowia coughing in one of the rooms. He also heard the swish of her merciless broom. The attic's candlelit air was hazy with swirling dust, and he hoped it didn't make them sneeze for half the night.

Then he risked going outside. For drinking water, he filled a wooden bucket at the well in the courtyard's center. For their meals, he sneaked into the kitchen three times to borrow clay plates and bowls, a pewter jug, and two pewter tankards. He also pilfered a few delicacies including *foie gras pâté* from the abbot's private pantry.

These private supplies would be missed, of course, but would the cook and his helpers report the theft? In their place, he would hide the robbery. The peevish abbot was likely to punish them for not safeguarding the pantry.

Besides the few delicacies, Bertwoin also took hard cheeses, day-old produce, cold chicken, and Minervois red wine along with four duck eggs. These were easier items to replace if the cook wished to conceal the thefts. He hoped this food and wine would impress Flowia.

Again in the attic, Bertwoin laid everything out on the floor around her. He then strutted to the trapdoor and dropped it in place with a flourish.

Flowia watched him with a satisfied little smile. "It still needs a good scrubbing, but I think our nest will do for us."

Bertwoin snapped his fingers. "Oh, I forgot."

He hurried to the next building and returned with a monk's black robe. He held it up by its sleeves in front of him. "For you, Brother Flowio. Now we both can feign monkish humility and hide our faces under cowls. We'll sleep most of the day here," he waved around the attic, "and wander where we will at night.

"Oh," he added, "I also want you to find me an herb that'll sicken a man until he retches and foams at the mouth." He raised a cautionary forefinger. "But it should not kill him."

Flowia cocked her head to one side. "Does the bold plowman mean to punish the abbot?"

He wiggled his eyebrows roguishly at her. "That should turn his thoughts away from us, should it not?"

She wobbled her head in disbelief, thought a moment, then said, "And you expect me to disturb/the dark forest at night/and hunt for your villainous herb/without the benefit of sunlight?"

How did she rhyme words so fast? "Can't you just go to the Devil's Doorstep and ask Satan to give it to you?" he joked. "Wouldn't sickening an abbot cause Him joy?"

"It's easier for me just to fetch it from my supplies at home."

"What's it called, this herb?"

Her expression turned blank. "It's a plant pigs learn early to avoid. It will cause demons to scamper inside the abbot's fat head."

He grunted. Like Brother Theodoric or Na Thea, Flowia wasn't one to share her knowledge of herbs.

"You need to hang the linen sheets over our doorways," she told him.

"Well, before I do, I must go out one more time."

"You are tempting fate, Brother Bertwoin."

"I must refill our bucket with water."

As Bertwoin ghosted down the covered walkway at the

end of the inner building nearest the church, a cold shiver trickled down his spine. Had the Devil just looked his way? He crossed himself and slipped into denser shadow along the wall.

Carrying his bucket, he crept to the passage's archway beside the church and looked out on the serene inner courtyard. He heard only the cree-cree of crickets calling to one another. No sandals flapped along the echoing gallery. No brothers walked under the trees or sat on the bench near the well.

Then Bertwoin heard one of the church's doors creak. He shoved his back against the rough stone wall and held his breath. *Please don't let them come this way.*

A man wearing a tunic stepped out of the church and hesitated. His head twitched about like a suspicious sparrow.

Bertwoin recognized Tolarto. Hatred flared through him. His hand dropped to his rope belt before he remembered he wore a brother's robe. He had replaced the knife stolen from him when he was arrested with one from the abbey, but he had left it behind in the attic.

Bertwoin stayed still as a rabbit. If he moved, he might draw the cur's eye. If the mule-whipper did come his way, he would thump him with the bucket, then escape through the church.

But Tolarto slunk away from Bertwoin, moving along the church's high wall like a furtive rat. He faded into the dark corridor leading toward the medicine garden.

Why was Tolarto lurking about inside the abbey? Was he meeting Brother Theodoric? He carried nothing, so he wasn't selling anything he had stolen off a mule's back.

Bertwoin decided to chance it. He gave Tolarto time to sneak all the way down the opposite passageway, then darted across the church's front and slipped into the dark walkway. It was empty, *Deo gratias*. He hurried to the end, again shoved his back against the wall, and peered out at Brother Theodoric's garden. No one was there.

A man cleared his throat just around the building's corner and startled Bertwoin. Hidden from sight, the man was only three arm lengths away. Bertwoin held his breath.

"In four days," Tolarto murmured. "After nightfall."

"Where?"

Bertwoin recognized the other voice. Tolarto had come to meet Brother Nigellus, the cursed monk who had put the *bayle* on his scent. So the two enemies he hated most were now meeting in secret.

"In the woods at the Widow's Altar," Tolarto said. "Near Drouet's place."

"Is Drouet a *credente*?"

"Hah, that would mean he'd have to give shelter to traveling Good Men. Drouet would charge his own mother for a bed or a meal."

"And you're certain Gertrude herself will be there?" Nigellus asked.

"Yeah, she's to do most of the preaching. But two Good Men are also coming. It'll be a fine catch for you, brother."

"We'll see. You never did explain to me why you showed yourself to the plowman that day? No one should ever connect the two of us."

"We weren't anywhere near each other," Tolarto growled.

"Why take such a risk? If you're not cautious, you'll lose your usefulness."

Tolarto grumbled, "I had business to attend to. I wanted to cut short your flirting with the little bitch."

"How dare you accuse me of flirting?" The monk's voice, though not much louder than a murmur, was shrill with outrage. "I was trying to rescue her soul."

"Hah, right. It must frustrate you, brother. Here you are

doing noble work, holy work, and everybody and their mules think they know what you really wanted from her."

There was a pause, then the monk asked with oily suspicion, "So, Tolarto, you say you were there before we arrived. You saw the plowman dance with the woodcutter's daughter. They argued, and he slapped her? And later, you saw him turn aside after searching for you and follow her in the forest?"

"Why do you doubt me, brother? I saw him slap her just before you and the saint showed up. After leaving you, he searched for me but couldn't find me, because I didn't want to be found. He had already gone off after in the woods by the time you came back to meet me."

"So Brother Gregorius and I walked past you without seeing you before we talked to Emeline?"

"It's a gift I have, brother. People only see me if I want them to see me. You were with holier-than-thou Gregorius, and I thought it prudent that he didn't see me, even if he is a monk. As you said, brother, we must be cautious."

"And you're telling me the truth? The plowman slapped Emeline?"

"I said it, didn't I?"

"You did, muleteer," said Brother Nigellus in a grating tone. "And I told the *bayle*. He thinks I saw Bertwoin slap her. He thinks I saw the plowman wander off into the forest. I made no mention of you. It would be a grave sin against my soul to bear false witness against him."

"If you find you don't want my information, I can take it elsewhere."

"I just want *truthful* information. Gertrude had better be at the meeting in four days. The abbot intends to inform the bishop. No one will believe me again if you're wrong."

"She'll be there," Tolarto muttered.

"She had better be. I won't suffer punishment without including you in it."

"Don't threaten me, black robe. You don't want to make an enemy of me. Now, do you have my money or not?" There was a pause, then Tolarto said cheerily, "Thank you, brother."

Bertwoin scurried away before Tolarto could enter the passageway and find him there. He darted into the nearest empty room along the gallery. After a few moments, he heard a church door creak open and close. So now Tolarto was gone. Bertwoin waited. Then Brother Nigellus shuffled past his room's open doorway as he returned to his cell.

When Bertwoin returned to the attic with a bucket of water, he found Flowia lying on her side on the main room's swept floor. When he dropped down opposite her, he smelled Minervois in a pewter tankard near her elbow.

Picking up a duck's egg, she sawed off the point of its shell with her dagger and drank the yolk and white in one gulp. Her expression turned dreamy.

"The abbot eats well," she purred. She watched him with a knowing smirk.

"What?" he asked.

"You want to tell me something, Brother Bertwoin."

"How do you know that?"

"You're as excited as a boy who just caught his first rabbit. What is it?"

"Tolarto is a Judas," he blurted out. He told her all he had heard and finished by saying, "He would sell his sister's soul to the Devil if it brought him profit. I know Tolarto's loose in his devotions, but is he not one of the Good Folk?"

Flowia stared at the taper's tiny flame. "So he says. He pretends to honor them while he betrays them. We must warn Gertrude tomorrow night."

CHAPTER XX.

ot long after vespers on the following night,
Bertwoin and Flowia sneaked out of their attic
hideaway with food for Gertrude. They were just
about to trespass into the abbey's vaulted church when a
monk with a bucket bouncing against his leg shuffled out of
the dark passageway leading to Brother Theodoric's medicinal garden.

Bertwoin prayed that the church was empty and jerked
open one of its front doors. He and Flowia—their faces
shielded by woolen cowls—darted inside before the monk
could call out to them.

The church was solemn and cool...and, *Deo gratias*, empty.
Bertwoin closed the door firmly behind them. They hurried
into the darkness beyond the glow of the welcoming candle
and hid. The brother with a bucket didn't follow them.

Flowia snickered when Bertwoin also let out his held
breath.

"With the sound of a boy
whooshing air from a pig's bladder
the plowman shows his wild joy
when the dark monk doesn't matter."

"How do you do that?" he asked.

"What?"

"Make up rhymes so fast?"

"Practice."

Bertwoin glanced at the Virgin Mary high up in her radiant stained-glass window. She sat adoring her sacred son, who looked down into the church with a wise and forgiving expression. Flowia was just as beautiful as the Virgin but not as serenely gentle.

He told her, "To the brother, we were just two pious monks going to pray/and now that he's gone, there's nothing more to say."

Flowia smiled. "When Gertrude sees two monks knocking on her door at night, her old heart will tremble. Anyone hiding under her house will pee all over themselves."

"Maybe I should lurk beside her cellar door and see who comes running out."

"If we do flush anyone out, there will be two of them," Flowia said. "To be safe, their female apostles always travel in pairs."

Bertwoin said in a more serious tone, "You say little Marthe now has the spitting-blood disease too?"

"Yes," Flowia said. "And I doubt any cure will save her."

"So Gertrude has lost a husband, a brother-in-law, a son, and all of her daughters except her youngest. Bishop Othon gloats because her disbelief brought this curse down upon her."

Flowia shook her head. "And the Good Folk argue otherwise. They say the Evil God who rules over the earth torments her because of her unstinting saintliness."

"Well," said Bertwoin, "we know that keeping her *ostal* and farm torments Bishop Othon."

Flowia muttered, "Everyone profits from Gertrude's situation except her."

He knew what she meant. Both the Church and Good Folk used Gertrude as an example, and Jean-Luc used her situation to benefit the domain. Since Gertrude had no men in her disease-smothered household, the *visconte* would normally have replaced her. He needed men to work his fields and to soldier for him. But Gertrude had a crowd of Good Folk men who willingly paid the labor she owed the *visconte*. And Sir Jean-Luc twisted their charity to his advantage. Instead of the toil of two or three men in her household, he contrived to work ten men on her behalf.

Bertwoin and Flowia kept to the forest, and so met no one on the way to Gertrude's cottage. Stripes of candlelight glowed in the slits between her shutter's slats. Instead of tossing pebbles against the shutter or rapping on it to announce their arrival, Flowia knocked on the pine door four times, paused, then three times, paused, then twice, paused, then once.

Bertwoin adjusted his cowl. Why was he surprised that Flowia knew the Good Folk's coded knock? She ministered to all who came to her and probably had visited many of them at night. So they trusted her with their secret, and now, she had decided to trust him.

Bertwoin whispered, "I'll never betray this."

Gertrude swung the door open on its leather hinges and took a half a step back when confronted by two black-robed monks. Seeing no one except Gertrude in the house, Flowia pulled back her cowl.

Gertrude relaxed. "Hah, it's you."

She nodded to Bertwoin when he pulled back his cowl but still eyed him with mistrust.

"You two almost scared the soul out of my body."

Bertwoin enjoyed listening to her melodious voice. Her preaching or singing would bring righteous joy to a congregation of *credentes*. Her black habit hung on her spare body as if from a peg, and she wore her gray hair long and loose, which gave her a wild look, as did the glare in her dark eyes.

The Church judged her feral appearance as a sign of her witchhood. She was also a weaver by trade, and the Church eyed weaving, though it was a necessary craft, with suspicion. To deter people from buying Gertrude's cloth, one local priest accused her of weaving secret, diabolical patterns into her work.

After Gertrude blessed them and thanked God for the bounty they had brought her, the three of them sat on the dirt floor around her small hearth. Its embers had already been covered with ashes, but she now added kindling and blew it back into flame. Her movements were quick and darting, reminding Bertwoin of a sparrow. Two hens in the kitchen eyed them with suspicion. Since Gertrude wasn't allowed to eat eggs, Bertwoin assumed little Marthe ate them.

Gertrude had taken up a beggarly life, as her house showed. It was as bare as a knothole. Her voluntary poverty impressed Bertwoin. If only gluttonous abbots, rich bishops, and the militant Pope also lived what they preached. Would the world not be a better place?

True, men and women caught fish for Gertrude, butchered winter meat to feed her last daughter, helped her harvest her crops, and did chores for her, but Gertrude, in turn, performed the spiritual duties necessary to comfort their rough lives, especially when they lay dying. She lived in the true spirit of the Biblical Apostles.

She did have a taper burning, but that was because she

had been sewing and needed its light. No doubt she often sat in the dark. He saw a crude table and wooden cooking utensils in the kitchen and a scarred pine trunk in the front room, but nothing else. With its stool and straw bed, his dungeon cell had been as well-furnished. He assumed her loom was in the cellar.

Flowia said, "Tolarto Malet told Brother Nigellus that you will preach at the Widow's Altar three nights from now."

For two breaths, Gertrude stared into a corner where the quivering fire threw trembling shadows. She sucked in her lips, then sighed. "So we too have our Judas. Thank you. I will warn the others that he means us harm."

"Will you punish him for betraying you?" Bertwoin asked.

"It will not change him. Evil is always with us. It is enough to know from whence it comes and to dodge it. From this day on, we will tell him only what we want the Church to know."

Flowia cleared her throat. "We have also come to ask you some questions about Emeline. The master needs information."

Gertrude laid another twig on her timid hearth fire. "Little Emeline was smart, charitable to all and devout, and was petite as an almond's flower. Considered forgoing marriage for the life of a Good Woman. Seemed to have the calling and had a stout heart." She swallowed. "She could have become either a Good Woman or a good wife to Sebastian."

Flowia asked, "Was Emeline still taking instruction from you?"

Gertrude nodded.

"So she wouldn't wear a cross?"

"Never. She was a true believer."

"And what of Brune?" Flowia asked.

Gertrude frowned. "You think she too...?"

Flowia raised her eyebrows. "She disappeared. Was not Brother Nigellus interested in saving her too?"

"Yes," Gertrude said slowly.

"What did Sebastian think of her visiting you?" Bertwoin asked gently.

Gertrude snorted and flipped her gray hair behind her. "We fought over her, didn't we? Like two dogs over a juicy rat. And maybe we both would have won."

When they waited in silence, she explained, "He would get her body and love now, and I would eventually get her soul. Didn't I follow that path myself?"

"And Villenc?" Bertwoin asked.

"That villain? He threatened to blind her, didn't he?"

"To me, that sounds like one given to torture," Bertwoin murmured. He grimaced at his *faux pas*. Why had he mentioned torture, a fate Roqua had also suffered?

A single tear dribbled down Gertrude's wrinkled cheek. "Those who are given to violence also suffer. They know no peace." She looked directly at Bertwoin. "I think your father also suffers like a bear with a thorn in its paw."

Flowia patted the widow's knobby hand and said, "Brother Nigellus also fought for Emeline's soul."

Gertrude spat into her fire. "And for her body. He was determined that she not go to her marriage bed a virgin. Emeline took care never to be alone with him."

Bertwoin frowned. He had seen Brother Gregorius shuffle toward Carcassonne while Nigellus had gone toward where Tolarto hid in the woods. How long had Tolarto and the monk talked? Either one of them might have stalked Emeline after their secret meeting. Was that why Tolarto had lied? Or did Brother Nigellus find it convenient to deflect suspicion away from himself?

"Did Emeline ever say she was afraid of anyone else?" he asked Gertrude.

"Not that I know of. She was no fool, that one, but she

did look for the thread of good in everyone. I even heard her praise Villenc once. Said he did the work of two men."

"Did she never mention Tolarto?"

"No. Why do you have him in your thoughts?"

"He dodged into the woods not far from us on the last day that I saw Emeline."

Gertrude said in a husky voice, "Emeline never said anything good or bad about him. Roqua didn't either."

Since Gertrude had brought up her daughter, Bertwoin asked quietly, "Was Roqua afraid of anyone?"

Gertrude yipped surprised laughter. "My Roqua didn't fear man, demon, or saint."

"Were Emeline and Roqua good friends?"

"They liked each other, but they had different lives and different friends. Emeline was younger and hadn't been married." She glanced from Flowia to Bertwoin and grinned. "Marriage matures you."

"Is that not a high price to pay for maturity?" Flowia asked. "And is it the only path?"

"Oh, it has its joys too." Gertrude glanced around at her bare house as if it were proof. "I only hope the souls of my Roqua and poor Emeline found worthy new lives."

Bertwoin raised a hand toward his forehead, caught himself before he made the sign of the holy cross, and scratched his cheek instead. Gertrude smiled. She knew what he had meant to do.

"At least with us, plowman, you have more chances to reach heaven."

"More chances?"

"Does the Church not tell you that this is the only life you will ever get?" she asked in her melodious voice. "Does your priest not say you have to be perfect in this one life or your spirit will not realize blessed peace when your body feeds the worms?"

He scowled and mumbled, "I haven't thought about it that much."

"Do you not think it harsh, plowman, for your God to give you only one chance to reach His heaven? And to demand the blood sacrifice of His Son before He gives you this single chance?"

Sudden anger burned in Bertwoin's chest. Wasn't he trying to find the murderer of her daughter? Why badger him with unanswerable questions? He was no priest armed with Bible learning.

"It's blasphemous," he snapped, "to ask me to judge God."

"Did God not give us the talent to reason?" She watched him with her head tilted to one side, sparrow-like. "It is not judging the Gods to ask the manner of their ways. If God is good and almighty, why does He allow evil to have sway in our world?"

"I'm a simple plowman. Ask Bishop Othon instead."

"And what will your bishop say?"

Bertwoin had no intention of swimming into that trap. He shrugged away her question.

"That no man can know the ways of the Lord," Flowia answered in his stead. "That God has His reasons for letting evil exist. And that one of His reasons is to test us."

Excited, Gertrude flapped her hands. "This is true. No man knows. Yet your priests pretend to know. They tell us what God intends and what He thinks and wants."

"And how do *you* answer this question?" Bertwoin challenged.

The age lines around Gertrude's eyes crinkled upward with her smile. "It's a simple teaching. One the Church finds alarming." She raised a forefinger to emphasize the importance of her coming words. "There are two Gods. One is good and rules the heavens. He created our souls. The other rules this world and created our bodies from primal clay. The Evil One rules over us here on Earth."

Bertwoin made the sign of the cross.

"We can never change the Evil God," she said, "or the ways of this world. But if we rise above evil, our spirits may finally fly home to reside with the Heavenly God."

Bertwoin stood up. Maybe it was true what people said: God allowed Gertrude to live so He could punish her for her disbelief. That explained why she had not caught the spitting-blood disease. Instead, like Job, she suffered mightily while all those she loved died.

"We must leave now," he announced.

Gertrude nodded with a bird-like twitch of her head. "'He who has ears to hear, let him hear.' I thank you, plowman, and you, Flowia, for bringing us food and drink. It will give strength to my little Marthe."

Bertwoin looked at this widow huddled by her fire as her last child lay dying. He said gently, "We are happy to help and will do so again."

She stared at her knobby hands. "Oh, how my Roqua did laugh. She came out of my womb smiling. I just knew she'd outlive me. But it was not to be."

Bertwoin felt as helpless as a legless cat. He couldn't relieve her grief.

They left Gertrude in her bare room. As they walked home under the light of an egg-shaped moon, Flowia asked, "So was Brune also killed by this fiend?"

"And were there others before her?" Bertwoin asked. "And does he only kill women?"

Flowia shook her fists in frustration. "Is Brother Nigellus the killer or just a connection between these young women?"

Bertwoin grunted. "Would a monk who says he wants to save their souls kill them so they cannot be saved?"

CHAPTER XXI.

As soon as they returned to their attic hideaway, Flowia began washing their common room floor with a wet cloth, smearing dust into mud before finally wiping up the filth and rinsing her rag in a bucket of dirty water.

Bertwoin leaned in the doorway of his room to block her from invading it with her ardor for cleaning. "So, Brother Flowio, you should be praised for doing so humble a task. Or is all of this cleaning a penance for some secret sin? Either way, you bring honor to your black robe."

She stood up and spread her arms wide to display the woolen glory of the robe that puddled around and hid her feet. "Like me, the robe is modest and well suited to scrubbing attic floors. And may I say that your laxity, Brother Bertwoin, bestows no honor on the robe you wear."

"I ponder more important things than floor dust," he said with a nobleman's sneer. "I ponder 'earth to earth, ashes to ashes, dust to dust.' I raise myself above the drudgery of this woeful world, the one Gertrude says is ruled by an Evil God."

She started to curtsy, then remembered that she wore a

monk's outfit and bowed instead. "I admire your *raised* nature. Still, since our brothers of the black robe are now sleeping between prayers, I think you should consider sneaking to the well in the courtyard and *raising* clean water for us."

Laughing, he picked up the wooden bucket. She began sweeping webs off the limestone walls with her broom, stabbing skittering spiders with its bristles as she went.

When he returned and set the bucket at her feet, she told him with a sad half-smile, "There's little respect among thieves."

"What?" He wondered what he had done wrong.

"I caught a bold rat the size of a squirrel nibbling on the baguette you stole from the kitchen. I think I shall call him Monsieur Larron and teach him to fetch things for us."

"Probably thinks it's a fair rent to charge us for invading *her* attic."

"Oh, it's definitely a *he-rat*."

"You're sure?"

"If I had two pearls that large, I could buy a *château*. He's the envy of all male rats and the sighing hope of all the females."

With downcast eyes, she shook her head. "It's my fate to associate with thieves on four legs and two. They are the company I keep now. How low I have fallen."

"Well, one expects a rat in a storeroom, right?"

"What about the other animals hiding here?" Flowia asked, still smiling.

Alarmed, Bertwoin glanced around. Had she seen a ghost? "What animals?"

"Well, for one, there's the prowling fox." Flowia raised her hands near the candle's soft glow, clasped them together, and twisted her fingers to form the shadow-head of a sharp-eared fox on a nearby wall.

Laughing, Bertwoin clapped. "Where did you learn this?"

"The wandering troupe of actors that bought me did teach me a few things."

After Flowia showed several animal shadows on the wall, she rose, picked up her bucket, shuffled to a corner with it, and thumped it down on the attic's plank floor.

A cry of surprise sounded on the storeroom landing below them. Bertwoin and Flowia froze like rabbits hearing the rustle of a weasel.

A voice below their feet shrilled, "What was that?"

"It's just the attic ghost," a deeper voice said.

"Hah. You believe that?" the first brother said.

"Do you not believe in the Holy Ghost?"

"Of course. We all do. But that's different."

"Is it?"

"The Holy Ghost is God."

Bertwoin crept to the trapdoor and stood on it so neither brother could push it open. Flowia tiptoed to their taper, licked her fingers, and pinched out the flame.

"You think Satan does not copy the Almighty for his own purposes?" the deeper voice asked. "Is Satan not depraved? Why should he not send malicious ghosts and demons to torment us?"

"It was probably just some animal."

"Keep telling yourself that. After you've been here for six months, you'll think otherwise."

"Then why has no one exorcised it? Why does our abbey tolerate an evil presence inside it?"

"Who knows? Perhaps the prior turns the wolf into his hound. Don't look at me like that. Evil might do good. The prior might use a restless ghost to guard his storehouse."

The first brother giggled. "It doesn't seem to work."

"Grab the dried fish," the deeper voice snapped. "A ghost finds a wall or floor no hindrance. You may tarry here if you wish and commune with it after I'm gone."

The voices faded as the brothers climbed down to the ground floor. Flowia and Bertwoin each hurried to separate crosses in the front wall and peeked outside. Three monks appeared in the moonlight, the hems of their black habits flapping as they rushed across the grassy strip between the inner buildings and their storehouse. Bertwoin frowned. Why had the third monk stayed silent?

In the dark lit only by moonlight lancing through the arrow slits, Flowia slapped his shoulder. "You knew of this ghost."

"You believe in such?"

"I trusted you."

"Flowia, I lived here for three days. There's no ghost. You don't need to fret about it."

"Do you not believe in them?"

"I didn't say that. My father saw the ghost of a dead crusader enter his tent after a battle. And he is not one given to lying. But this attic is empty save for us." He stopped himself from glancing around to make sure nothing glowed in the dark. "Why should I warn you of something that doesn't exist?"

Flowia put her hands on her hips. "The rumor must have arisen from some seed. Everything comes from something. Even Adam came from clay."

"Yes. And at least one of those three monks will now tell others they heard the ghost. That doesn't mean his tale is true."

"They also might keep quiet. They weren't fetching fish for the abbey's kitchen."

"Of course, that's why I didn't hear the third monk speak. He stood guard at the door while the other two slipped inside to pilfer fish." Bertwoin tapped a knuckle against his front teeth. "But why didn't we hear them enter the storeroom? What if I had jumped down and dropped into their laps?"

He scratched his scalp. "Well, I guess we can do without my slipping into the church to relight our candle."

"You can slip me back to my *ostal*, Brother Bertwoin. I will give you a sickening herb for the abbot's next meal."

"I can wait."

"But I have medicinal plants that can't. I need to attend to them. And I want to fetch a flint and fire-steel so we can light our candles here."

"Why didn't we go there right after seeing Gertrude?"

"Because I thought this attic was the safest refuge for us. That was before I came to understand that after dark, my home is less dangerous."

He doubted that he would change her mind. "So you're willing to help me punish Abbot Jehan?"

Flowia's voice in the dark was grim and merciless. "The abbot deserves to suffer here on Earth for his sins, not just later in Hell. He has the authority to punish you for trespassing in his abbey. Everyone grants him that. But he doesn't have the right to murder you for crimes you didn't commit, especially if he knows you didn't commit them."

Bertwoin grunted. "Well, while you're at your *ostal*, I'll slip off to my house. *Maman* is sure to be worried about me."

"Will she still be awake?"

"Probably. They usually wake up about now. With the grain harvests in and most of the threshing done, they're not too tired to get and repair tools before going back to bed until dawn."

"And since I went missing after I helped you escape," Flowia said, "she will wonder if we're together."

"She'll think I'm better off in your company," he lied. He had no intention of mentioning Flowia to his family. His *maman* would worry even more. It was said the alchemist's virgin could enchant men and turn them into pigs. This was nonsense, of course, but his *maman* might think there was a reason people said such things about her. "We should go now, before matins and return before lauds."

"Your family will not be wanting me there," Flowia said. "I'll wait at my house for you."

"I'm not sure how they feel about you," he lied.

"I am."

CHAPTER XXII.

A fter Bertwoin left Flowia in her dark and forlorn house, he trekked to his parent's home.

There, he pushed open the door and surprised his *maman*, father, and Uncle Laurence sitting in their fire-lit kitchen. They were drinking from bowls, and the bitter ale's malty scent gave Bertwoin the familiar and safe feeling of being home.

His *maman* rushed to him and hugged him. "Are you well?"

"Yes." He looked over her shoulder at his father and uncle, who were both grinning.

"Well, boy, you're going to be the talk of the diocese," his father bellowed. "Tweaked the bishop's long nose, didn't you? Gave your mother quite a shock, though. She carried food to the dungeon for you, and they told her you'd escaped."

His *maman* pulled him to a bench set against the kitchen's stone wall, and sat him beside his rangy uncle, who shook his hand to congratulate him. Picking up an earthen jug, she filled a bowl with dark, syrupy ale. "Have you eaten?"

"Like an abbot at high table."

His father slapped his thigh and guffawed. "Well, you're

dressed to resemble one. I took you for a monk or priest at first. Will you bless us, father?"

"Clanoud!" his wife scolded. She made the sign of the cross to protect them from his blasphemy.

Bertwoin signed an airy cross in the direction of his father. God would know he meant no blasphemy. "May you be blessed, poor sinner that you are."

"Bertwoin!" his *maman* cried. Again she crossed herself.

Laughing, his uncle slapped Bertwoin's shoulder. His *maman* began snapping the pointy ends of green beans and jerking them downward, stripping the stringy seams from their pods. Then she snapped the pods in half and tossed them into a large chestnut bowl on the table.

Flush with ale, his father crowed, "Some are saying the master spirited you away. Hilario swears he saw you fly over the Aude, riding behind the alchemist's virgin on a broom. Our priest is sure to claim a demon took you." Clanoud's expression turned somber. "We're told Flowia did visit you, and that she disappeared too."

Bertwoin didn't need to see the slight shake of his *maman's* head to know he should be wary. "It was her who did the trick that unlocked the dungeon's door."

His uncle glared at him. "Moors are full of tricks. Just remember, boy, your father fought the heathens in the Holy Land. None will ever sit under this roof. Don't bring ruin down on us, Bertwoin. Don't sin against the luck of our *ostal*."

Bertwoin glanced at his parent's bedroom where his father kept fingernail clippings from both his father and mother for luck. "I'd never sin against the spirit of our household or dishonor the memory of my grandfather or grandmother."

Bertwoin realized his hands were fists on the table and relaxed them. "And Flowia is not a Moor. She's as Christian as you are."

His uncle snorted. "Her skin says otherwise."

His *maman* told Bertwoin, "A boy came for you carrying a message from Michel Azema. Your father can tell you what he said."

Bertwoin twitched a brief smile, thanking her for changing the subject. "The boy told *you* what Michel wanted *me* to know?"

Clanoud wiggled his scarred fist. "You think I can't get a *boy* to talk?"

Bertwoin shook his head at his own stupidity. "How could I ever have doubted you?"

"I don't know." Clanoud sipped his ale. "Michel wants you to find what he left behind. He said to remember that half of what you earn from it is his."

His father studied him, searching for a clue to the meaning of Michel's words so he might learn what profit this would bring him.

Bertwoin had little trouble looking confused. "What Michel left behind was a little bag of seeds. He gave them to Brother Theodoric, who probably has already planted them. And I'm not bold enough to raid the abbey's herb garden."

"God forbid," his *maman* exclaimed.

"Michel says," his father continued, still watching him, "that whatever it is you are to find lies twelve paces south of the marked rowan."

"Well, Michel is ever full of mischief. Maybe the riddle has no answer. That means he can sit in his shepherd's *cabane* at night and laugh at me, knowing I'm scratching my head and trying to solve this little puzzle he left behind."

His uncle nodded. "Even when young, that boy had the ways of an outlaw in him."

His father leaned toward Bertwoin. "And you saw Michel give the monk these seeds?"

"I did." Bertwoin knew the silver denier he had earned for guiding Michel into the abbey was now at risk.

"And where was this? Why would you be with Michel?"

Bertwoin ignored the first question because his father knew he always earned a fee, either in coin or trade, for sneaking forbidden fruits into the abbey. The monks paid well and rightfully so. The abbey had eyes everywhere, so only Bertwoin and a few others dared smuggle contraband into it.

He told his father, "Ah, I don't know why, but Michel thinks I'm his true friend."

"Well," Clanoud muttered, "you're a clever one. If you solve it, I'll want to know."

"Of course. No matter what Michel expects from me, I'll need your help."

"You're right there. We all know you have the habit of wanting to give profitable things away. Like a suckling pig, for example."

Bertwoin sipped his ale, closed his eyes, and savored its malty flavor. "I'd rather find Emeline and Roqua's killer than the answer to Michel's riddle."

His uncle ran a fingertip slowly around the rim of his bowl. "It's said someone found one of Villenc's hammers near where Emeline drowned."

Bertwoin shook his head. "If so, Villenc dropped it there when he went to see where Emeline was found. Or the killer put it there to point blame at him."

"Villenc says it was stolen from him." His uncle's tone suggested he doubted this.

Bertwoin told him, "No hammer was there when I searched the area soon after her murder."

Then his uncle said with satisfaction, "Shit-brained Perter Sabatier has run off to tend sheep." He grinned at Clanoud. "But we expect the pig-butcher to come down the mountain soon and meet us on market day, don't we, brother?"

Bertwoin hesitated, not understanding what Perter's

running away had to do with Villenc. He glanced at his father, who waved the matter away. "Éléonore pestered us like a fly on stink. I couldn't get a moment's peace, what with your mother siding with her and nagging me all day. So I told them I'd forgo cracking the piss-bucket's skull if he came back and apologized like a man for hitting Wilfraed." Clanoud smirked. "He's to do it in full view of everyone on market day."

Bertwoin shook his head. "Perter gives Wilfraed an unwarranted blow, and innocent Éléonore suffers more for it than the bastard pig-butcher does."

His mother nodded agreement. "That's what I said."

His father rolled his eyes. "Ellyn, don't you start. It's done. Over with."

Bertwoin drained his bowl of ale. "Well, I should leave. This house is not safe for me or for you when I'm in it. Clerics and monks are sure to search for me here."

His uncle snickered. "Already have. And one of them went home with a black eye to match the color of his robe." He again slapped Bertwoin's shoulder. "Like son, like father. Now that smacking brothers is our family sport, I'll have to find me one and bloody his nose for him."

Clanoud leaned back, grinning. "I'll not have a black robe doubt my word in my own house."

When his *maman* hugged him and asked if he needed anything, Bertwoin told her, "No, *Maman*, I'm eating like a nobleman's favorite dog."

"Well, boy," his uncle said, "make certain that rich food doesn't turn you soft."

"They'll never gut the peasant out of me."

CHAPTER XXIII.

The coming day was still a faint, glowing promise when Janus checked his long line. He had baited twenty-five hooks on his nettle-hemp line the night before and stretched it across the brooding Aude.

His sister, Thea, had told him he must use either seven or sixteen or twenty-five iron or bone hooks if he wanted the saints to bring him good fortune. To draw even more good luck to himself today, he had also slathered his ragged tunic and wiry body with a gelatinous paste made from a rotten carp.

He untied one end of the nettle-hemp line he had looped around the slender trunk of a young elm that teetered on the weedy edge of the water. He gently let his line slip back into the cold, dark Aude. The river's grasping current sucked the braided line slithering from his hands.

Janus hurried barefoot over the wooden bridge and down the opposite bank to where he had tied the other end of his line around the trunk of an ash. Two empty reed baskets waited under the ash tree. His line slanted taut, pulled down-stream by the river's powerful undertow. Janus stepped ankle-deep into the chilly water and began pulling in his line, calloused hand over calloused hand.

His spirits rose at the weight of the line's pull. Saints Peter and Andrew had smiled down upon him. His sister would have many fishes to sell today. He would also salt or smoke some of this catch for the fair coming to Bourg in ten days.

He paused to swipe insects away from his face. The paste also brought this stinging plague, but luck was well worth a little irritation.

The taut line vibrated with thrashing fishes and eels. He kept his movements slow and smooth so he wouldn't jerk any fishes off their hooks. The current felt unusually powerful this morning. It must have rained in the high mountains yesterday or early during the night.

An animal moved in the woods behind him, probably a foraging pig or noisy squirrel, and he ignored it. He brought up the first hook, empty with its bait gone. Luck had smiled on some eel or fish during the night. The water swirled as his second hook neared the surface, and his spirits rose. It looked long enough to be an eel.

"So, old thief, now you do your own work instead of interfering in mine."

Janus stood paralyzed. It was not uncommon for Guillaume or his sons to be out hunting corpses just before daybreak, but even so, a chill shivered up Janus's spine.

If he brought up a fish now, or worse, a more expensive eel, the drowned-finder might demand it as additional payment for the fee he had lost on Emeline's corpse.

Janus turned and smiled. "D-did you have a f-find today?"

Guillaume stood haughty as an emperor with his legs spread and his arms crossed over the chest of his dark tunic. His smile, though, was less regal than menacing. "Oh yes, my luck has turned as sweet as honey."

"Did you wa-want a fish?"

"I think I want the fisherman instead."

Janus breathed slowly to settle his thrashing thoughts. To free his hands, he bent and let his line sink in the shallow brown water.

The drowned-finder stood directly behind him, blocking his way back onto land. Even as a boy of ten, Guillaume had enjoyed blinding geese or catching and gutting live cats.

Janus backed knee-deep into the river, its undercurrent tugging at his splayed feet and knobby ankles. He took two side steps downstream with the idea of going around Guillaume. Smiling like a wolf in the gray light, the damned whoreson took two steps down the bank to stay opposite him.

Guillaume chuckled. "You'll not steal away my fee this time, devil's meat. Not the one I'll get for finding your crooked corpse." His expression became beseeching. "I must do this. You do understand that, don't you? Otherwise, anyone will think he can claim the finder's fees that should come to me and mine."

Janus backed away. Cold water swirled around his groin, and he gasped. He glanced behind him. "Th-this will c-come between you and G-God," he pleaded.

The drowned-finder tested the water's temperature with a bare toe. He sighed, as if he regretted the work ahead of him, and stepped into the river. "They should give me a reward for ridding St. Vincent of a stinking dunghill like you. And don't worry," Guillaume added, "I'll not let the fishes you caught today go amiss. My woman will make a fine stew from them. And maybe I'll sell one or two of them to your sister. Then Ugly Thea will also see a profit from your night's catch. My sons will enjoy the joke in that."

Janus plunged downstream in a frantic effort to flank the

villainous drowned-finder, but Guillaume sidestepped to stay between him and the bank while also moving closer.

Janus pulled his sheathless fishing knife from his belt.

Guillaume hesitated for half a breath, then dismissed the threat with a mocking flip of a hand. "Do you think to gut me like one of your fish, dribble-mouth?"

With slow care, as if he didn't want to startle Janus, the drowned-finder waded a step closer, then another and another. He was well experienced in drowning men and women who carried knives.

Janus lashed at him with his blade. But Guillaume flinched backward just beyond the knife's tip. He then lunged forward while Janus still fought the river's grip and was momentarily twisted off-balance. Janus threw himself backward, then thrust his feet against the riverbed and came up slashing.

But Guillaume clubbed his thin arm aside with a forearm. Chuckling, he grabbed Janus's tunic, slick with rotted paste. Janus squirmed out of his grasp and plunged neck-deep in the water. Guillaume took a hesitant step toward him.

Janus, scared as he was, smiled. He had reached water high enough to be dangerous even to the taller drowned-finder. Now he was the one with experience. Janus ducked his head below the surface and began walking downstream underwater along the river's bumpy bottom.

After six strides, he turned back and shoved through the soft water toward the bank. When his head rose dripping above the surface, he saw that Guillaume had waded closer to the bank to stay between him and land.

"You're damned, devil's meat, damned," Guillaume roared. "I'll not let an ass-crack like you escape me. Come to me, and let's be quick about it. Come to me."

"You're Hell-b-bound yourself, you s-son of a wh-whore,"

Janus taunted. "Your m-mother w-worked at the p-public baths."

Guillaume snarled and came for him.

Janus glanced behind him. The sun's brow was now above the far mountains and threw blessed light shimmering across the water's surface. If only someone would hear or see them. But no one was in sight.

He was slippery as a greased eel. Would that give him the advantage he needed to slice open the drowned-finder's belly? No, the spiteful knave was too experienced at this.

Janus bit his lower lip. He was already a third of the way across the river. Could he reach shallow water on the other side?

He turned his back on the drowned-finder and waded deeper. Just before his head slipped below the cold surface, he heard the Guillaume yell, "I'll drink to your death with the fee I get for your body, you shriveled, stinking fish shit."

Janus walked down into the depths, down into an underwater dimness where a flat ceiling of radiant light hung above him. He kept his strides slow and measured and long to conserve his breath yet also to cover the riverbed as quickly as possible.

He stepped into space. Startled, he flailed his arms before holding them straight down his sides as he drifted further into the depths until his bare feet thumped against the sandy bottom. The water's weight pressed against his eardrums.

Please, Saint Peter, he prayed, *protect a brother fisherman. Save me.*

The relentless current muscled him downstream. He used the current's direction to reorient himself and continued to shove his way toward the opposite bank.

Keep calm, keep calm. Walk, don't try to swim.

His throat ached, but he couldn't let it relax. It must stay corked to keep breath in his chest. Then he stumbled off another ridge and flapped his arms to stay upright as he sank deeper. The current swept him downstream. He kicked his feet, trying to propel himself in the direction of the bank.

His heart pounded, and his lungs pulsed and gasped for the light-filled air far, far above him. He again felt the river's solid bottom below his feet but doubted he would make it now. Would the water carry him too far downstream for the whoreson to find him? Would that even matter?

Flashes flared at the edges of his eyes. Then a bright spot appeared and widened until all he could see was radiant cold light.

CHAPTER XXIV.

Two nights after Bertwoin visited his *ostal*, he and Flowia again sneaked out of the abbey. As they approached the master's house, they saw light glowing between the slats of the front shutter. Flowia danced forward a step or two.

When she started to run toward the opening in the mulberry hedge, Bertwoin grabbed her arm and whispered, "It might be someone else. Maybe a trap."

He leaned toward the cottage to listen. Crickets near the spring chanted love poetry, and faraway, a dog barked.

Bertwoin crept to the mulberry hedge, slipped through its opening like a shadow, and tiptoed to a shutter. The hearth fire's faint glow shone on the kitchen's stone walls. The master sat at the table, playing chess, with bread and a copper goblet within reach.

When Bertwoin waved Flowia forward, she ran to the front door and flung it open. He tarried outside a moment to give them privacy before he went in and found Flowia already tidying up her kitchen.

The alchemist looked well pleased to see him. "So, plowman, you and Flowia are still free to roam the night. You must have chosen your hiding place well."

"It serves. Did you have a good journey, master?"

"It was rewarding in its own way." He waved Bertwoin to a three-legged stool across the table.

Bertwoin closed the door and smiled at Flowia. She poured dark ale into a pewter tankard and set it on the table beside him. He hoped she still intended to return to the attic with him.

The old goldsmith eyed him, then Flowia. He wiped a breadcrumb off the tabletop. "The noble master I visited was able to show the presence of fat in the debris under Emeline's fingernails. So the fragment of thread was wool, not hemp or linen. That, along with the fact that the killer probably wore sandals, is telling. I think, Bertwoin, you will have to sneak me into the abbey one more time. Tomorrow night will be best."

"The abbey?" Flowia asked. "Won't that be dangerous?"

"Yes," the alchemist admitted. "But I think it necessary. Tomorrow, during the day, I will visit Prior Simon. His answers will determine if we can forgo this visit or not." He rubbed his chin. "I still wonder why the killer doesn't commit his crimes during daylight when his fire is sure not to be seen."

Bertwoin thought they had already discussed that. "During daylight, some people are brave enough to pass near the Devil's Doorstep. Even fishermen wait for sunrise before going near it."

The old man nodded. "This means our murderer does not fear the Devil. And speaking of fishermen, have you heard that Janus is missing?"

Flowia whirled to face him. "Janus?"

"Yes, daughter." His expression resigned, he took a sip

from his goblet. "And I fear that if anyone does find him now, there will be a fee in it for them."

"He drowned?"

The alchemist hummed assent. "Rumor has it that Guillaume tried to drown him like an unwanted pup. But he wriggled out of Guillaume's grasp, and the current took him. The drowned-finder and his surly sons hunted both banks for the corpse but never found it. Nor has anyone else so far. The fee stands untaken."

"How would anyone know Guillaume tried to kill him?" Bertwoin asked.

"Ah well, somebody witnessed it."

Bertwoin frowned. "It's not like Guillaume to be so careless. Has the *bayle* arrested him?"

The alchemist's lips puckered in disgust. "He pretends not to know anything about this matter. And the witness is no fool. Since he or she has not yet openly reported this crime to the *bayle*, Guillaume doesn't yet know the name of his accuser."

"But the witness told the story to someone," Flowia argued. "Otherwise we would know nothing of it."

"You would have to know who first related the rumor to know who saw the deed done." He rubbed his thin hands together. "And who can tell the true origin of a rumor?"

Bertwoin shrugged. "This was bound to happen. Janus gave Guillaume part of the fee he got for finding Emeline, but no way was the drowned-finder going to accept competition."

Flowia said, "A wise woman foretold that water would be the death of old Janus and also that it would be his unmarked grave."

They sat a moment in silence and considered the mysterious ways of the world until Flowia told the master, "Speaking of unmarked graves, we think Brune was also one of the killer's victims. We talked with Gertrude, but she told us little about Brune." She then told him about their visit to Gertrude.

The alchemist picked up a small black piece and studied it. "These young women are just pawns in his game, and they are also treated as such by the churchmen. The bishop and abbot both claim the killer is one of the Good Folk." He nodded at Flowia. "And yes, daughter, Brune also fits the pattern of this killer's victims. Ah well, you both had better go. Our enemies will know I have returned. They may think you silly enough to welcome me back. Though I am well pleased that you did."

The alchemist placed the piece he had picked up back on the board. "So, plowman, tomorrow I want you to sneak into the abbey after compline while the monks are in their cells and unlock a little-used door somewhere. Then meet me on the bridge just before matins. We will sneak into the abbey while the brothers and clerics busy themselves praising God."

When Bertwoin got up, he glanced down and saw a long strand of Flowia's hair on the tabletop. It lay with its upper end twisted in a circle that crossed over the straight base, forming a supple rood. Gooseflesh pimpled the backs of his upper arms. Was this a premonition of danger? Did this hair, this cross, foretell the coming of the *bayle*? Or were the monks even now on their way?

Flowia stuffed a few things in a hemp sack, kissed the master's cheek, and they hurried away.

At the wooden bridge, Bertwoin turned away from St. Vincent and headed toward the Devil's Doorstep.

Flowia followed him eight or ten paces before she stopped. "Why are we heading away from the abbey?"

"The fox doesn't run straight to its lair."

She glanced around. "Are we being followed?"

"Not that I know of. Truth be told, I'm going in this direction because I need your help to solve a riddle."

"Oh," she said with sudden interest, "a riddle?"

"Yeah, sent to me by an outlaw shepherd. Not long before Emeline was murdered, Michel had me sneak him into the abbey. He gave Brother Theodoric a small pouch of seeds."

"And what do they grow?"

"The monk told me the plants heal burns."

"A rare gift indeed."

Bertwoin stopped a moment to listen to the night and the river behind them. He then shrugged away the feeling of being watched, and they walked on.

"Anyway," he whispered, "I understand Lopside's bray better than I do the meaning of Michel's message. I am to find something twelve paces south of a certain rowan tree. Michel carved a cross on it when we were boys together."

Bertwoin slowed as they neared the Devil's Doorstep. Just before they came within sight of the haunted place, he turned off the pathway and pointed at a rowan a stone's throw from where they stood.

"That's the one." He marched to the tree and circled it. "And there's the cross. It's lower than I thought."

"You were a boy, Brother Bertwoin. And trees grow from their tops, not up from their roots."

"Thank you, Brother Flowio, but even a simple peasant like me knows how a tree grows."

"Well, how do I know what you know and what you don't know?" she asked, getting in the last word as usual.

Bertwoin turned and stepped off twelve paces to the south. "This is where I'm supposed to find something. All I see are trees, underbrush, and shadows in the moonlight." He frowned down at a square of recently turned dirt half a step from his monk's sandal.

Flowia pointed at a group of nearby plants. "They're called rooster of the garden. I'm going to remember this spot. Their tea has many uses."

"Like not having babies?" Bertwoin muttered.

"Yes, that's one of its functions." She looked him up and down, from cowl to sandals. "Interesting that you would know that particular benefit."

Bertwoin squatted beside the square of disturbed dirt. "I also happen to know that tansy and hairy pennyroyal used together will end a pregnancy."

Flowia put her hand to her mouth. "Oh, I forgot to fetch the herb you wanted for the abbot's supper."

He shrugged. "It'll wait."

Bertwoin stared down at the square. Tiny new weeds covered its surface like fur. He began digging with his monk's dagger, piling the loose dirt along one side. He dug an elbow-deep hole without finding anything, then stood up to relieve the ache in his calves and knees.

He shook his head. "I don't understand. Whatever it is, it can't be that deep."

Flowia looked from the hole to the loose dirt piled on one side of it and cocked her head. "What's that?"

"What? The dirt?"

"No. What's that growing in it?"

Bertwoin shrugged. "Weedlings."

"There's no such thing as a weed," she said. "God doesn't make useless things. Everything has its use, good or bad."

"Thanks for the sermon, Brother Flowio, but that doesn't explain the riddle."

She pointed at a few sprouts prickling the pile of loose dirt. "What are these plants?"

Bertwoin waved at the hushed forest around them. "How would I know? You're the expert, so you tell...." He smacked his forehead with his palm. "That sly fox." Squatting again, he brushed some dry dirt off a hair-like seedling.

Flowia put her hand to her mouth, her eyes wide. "This

could be a great boon for us. Did Michel name these seeds he brought to Brother Theodoric?"

"No, and Brother Theodoric didn't name them either. He only said they healed burns." Bertwoin held up a finger gritty with dirt. "I think they may be something that Brother Flowio, the renowned healer, might make use of."

He then shook his head in wonder. "I've been as dense as ash wood. How could I not have guessed that Michel would steal a few seeds from the pouch? He's as curious as a crow. He must have planted some of them even before we visited Brother Theodoric so he would learn what grew from them."

Flowia hummed disagreement. "You're too kind in your opinion, Brother Bertwoin. Greed more than curiosity afflicted Michel's heart. He wanted to sell them as medicine."

She watched Bertwoin, considering him.

"What?" he asked.

"A thief believes everyone else is also a thief. Yet Michel believes you're so honest you'll give him half of what you earn without his watching over you. It's either a compliment or he had no other choice."

"I expect to earn a good profit from these seedlings even if the crop fails. Michel gave me a coin, but he also owes me some wool for sneaking him into the abbey, a debt I never expected to collect. But now he has to visit me if he wants to see any reward from this theft. Even if he sends a boy to collect the profit for him, I'll not pay until I have his gift of wool in my hands. And even if these seedlings wither, I'll not let Michel know of it before he brings me the wool he owes me."

Flowia squatted beside Bertwoin and began sifting seedlings out of the dry dirt and setting them aside. "We'll replant them here," she said, excited, "and tend those that survive. They're more valuable than any fleece if they soothe burned skin and heal flesh."

She picked out a seedling and held it up in the moonlight. "So does this herb produce fruit? Does its leaf make a salve for burns, or must I use some other part of the plant? Do I have to harvest it under a full moon?"

"Ask Brother Theodoric. But we both know he's not one to reveal his secrets."

She smiled sweetly. "Brother Theodoric is known to boast a bit after taking strong ale. Much of his good reputation comes from *his* telling other people what they should think of him."

Bertwoin remembered the master saying women were shrewd judges of men's characters. "Do you know all of our faults?"

"If you were to share a few drinks with Brother Theodoric, you might learn the secret of these seeds. And in the meantime, I will talk to those he heals with this medicine and see what I can learn."

As Bertwoin began filling the hole again, Flowia patted his broad back. "Let me know when you smuggle other things into the abbey for Brother Theodoric. He will never miss a few seeds or a cutting or two."

She stood up and skipped a joyous step.

"Oh, you picked the best place
on that we can both agree
when you hid us away from the chase
in the attic of the monks' abbey."

She bent and kissed his cheek bristling with a day-old beard. He smiled, feeling warm all over.

Flowia watched him work a moment. "Careful," she chided. "Let me do it." She knelt beside him and gently shoved him away.

He watched her replant the precious medicinal seedlings with precision.

When she finished and stood up, she frowned and whispered, "I feel as if someone is watching us."

They stood as still as rooted trees but heard only the normal noises of a night forest. Finally, Flowia picked up her hemp bag, and Bertwoin led her away from the rowan. To avoid the Devil's Doorstep, he took a circuitous route that brought him to an open field. After crossing it, he stopped in a copse on the other side to watch their trail. He too had felt a presence. But they spied nothing following them.

When they had passed the mill and were in sight of the abbey, he grunted.

"What?" she asked.

"Nothing much," he said. "I was just thinking that now we'll have to sneak out often to water and care for these seedlings. All because an outlaw shepherd laid this task on me. People like him always leave work behind for others to do."

"True." She tapped Bertwoin's forearm. "But remember, it was Michel who brought these seeds to Brother Theodoric. Because of him and you, I may soon bring a modicum of relief to those scalded by water or burned by fire."

She raised her fists and waggled them in joy. "The master knows many of nature's ways and wrings cures from plants that even Brother Theodoric cannot do. And maybe someday you will bring someone to the abbey who carries seeds that cure the spitting-blood disease. Through Michel and his kind, God may allow us to heal our sick and injured. Even Brother Theodoric thinks it wise to do business with a sinner like Michel."

AS BERTWOIN SETTLED ON HIS CRINKLY MATTRESS, FLOWIA dragged her mattress into his dark room and laid it out beside him. Surprised, he hesitated a moment before boldly scooting over to hers. Her hair smelled of rosemary. She pressed against his chest. He found her mouth with his thumb and gently brush-kissed her.

He thanked Rixende, the servant girl who was now the mistress of Montredon's randy priest, and who had taught him how to make love like a man instead of an animal.

Bertwoin let his kisses become longer and more ardent. Flowia followed his lead. He reached under her robe and began exploring her marvelous body, so soft yet so firm. He restrained his pulsating desire to possess her, keeping his manner slow and gentle.

Later, as Bertwoin lay relaxed with his arms around her warm body, his right leg over her firm thighs, he asked, "Will the master punish you for this?"

"Because I'm not a virgin?" She chuckled. "When Mary Magdalene was maybe fourteen years old, her father sent her by caravan across the desert to marry a rich trader. Bandits raided the caravan. She was carried off as a slave and sold in Babylon. Do you think she was still a virgin when she reached the city? Do you think she was a virgin when she later met Jesus and became one of his disciples?"

"You're *sure* she was a disciple?"

"Yes. And an important one too. She discovered His empty tomb. She was the first to see Jesus arisen as Christ."

"Why are we talking about her?"

After a moment's hesitation, Flowia asked, "Do you think I was a virgin for long after I was sold away at the age of thirteen?"

"Oh."

"Few things change in this world, Bertwoin, even after twelve hundred years."

How many times had they raped her? He unclenched his fists and pushed the thought out of his mind. No wonder she appreciated the fatherly alchemist. "And the master knew this when he paid for you?"

"He has lived long, learned well, and traveled. No one can call him a fool. He knew me for what I was."

Bertwoin grunted. "But many say he needs a virgin to make his magic work."

"Yes, and they also say he changes lead into gold." Flowia skimmed a fingertip along the ragged lines of healed boar scars on his chest. "The virgin is inside *him*." When Bertwoin tensed, she said, "Yes. It's confusing and complicated. I don't understand much of what he tells me, but I know having a woman in the house somehow helps him do his work. He told me that men like him are of many parts, and a spirit woman lives inside him. My helping him with his work brings forth this virgin inside him. He says she makes him whole. This virgin spirit cleanses his soul."

Bertwoin made the sign of the cross. He hoped God didn't let the abbot catch them as a punishment for Flowia's blasphemous words.

She laughed. "Yes, I felt the same when he first told me this. But he says it's in the Bible. In the beginning, a man was both male and female."

Again Bertwoin crossed himself. "Maybe we shouldn't talk about this."

She laughed, disentangled herself from his embrace, and got up. "I don't understand it well enough to talk about it anyway."

He asked, disappointed, "You're going to sleep in your own room now?"

She giggled. "No. I brought medicine with me to prevent my having a child."

So she had planned on their sleeping together? And why hadn't he seen even a hint of this coming?

CHAPTER XXV.

B ertwoin thought of his previous night with Flowia as
he watched the bridge from a riverside copse. Finally,
he saw the stooped figure of the goldsmith. The
moon glared straight above him, and no one, not even a fisherman, was in sight. So Bertwoin pulled the woolen cowl over
his head and shuffled out to meet him.

"Well, plowman, were you able to unlock a door for us?"

"Yes, master."

"Good. So again we trespass into the abbey's grounds. I
think we have a fine night for it. Let us hope you do not have
to punch another monk in the face."

Bertwoin flapped his right hand as if shaking away pain.
"How is it that a monk's soft nose could have stung my
knuckles so?"

"Yes, it was rude of his nose to cause you such suffering,"
the master said as they turned to walk along the river toward
St. Vincent. He raised an eyebrow. "I have learned that wasn't
the only harm you did the monks. They swarmed onto Drouet's land. He thought perhaps they were hunting you. But we

know, don't we, that they hoped to capture Gertrude and some of her flock? She owes her freedom to you and Flowia."

The mention of Flowia sent a thrill through Bertwoin. He raised his arms in celebration toward the half-moon. "There's joy in that."

"Yes, now Brother Nigellus will no longer trust Tolarto. The monk paid for information he thinks was a lie. And his superiors will be less than pleased with him."

Bertwoin remembered the hair cross on the table and glanced around. "Did your visit with Prior Simon go well, master?"

"Yes, more so than I had hoped. I believe guilt made him eager to give me all the information I wanted."

"Guilt?"

"Yes. He readily told me which cells belonged to Brothers Nigellus and Gregorius."

"You think it was one of them?"

Ignoring the interruption, the goldsmith continued, "I asked him whether any of the abbey's silver crosses, the ones they sell to pilgrims or put on corpses, had gone missing."

"Corpses whose families can *pay* for them," Bertwoin said.

"Prior Simon verified the theft of a number of them." The alchemist counted on his fingers as he said, "So we have sandal prints, evidence the killer wore dark wool, and silver crosses stolen from the abbey."

"But the monks and clerics here attend prayers every few hours during the night."

"Yes, which argues against our theory."

"Maybe we're not considering all the answers. Brother Nigellus might have given the silver crosses to Tolarto in payment. The muleteer wears sandals and woolen tunics. Or someone might have stolen the crosses and sold them to the killer. Or one of the village priests might have done it."

"Well thought, plowman. We must find out which monk or cleric stole roods from the abbey."

"How?"

"Our murderer may have a telling weakness." When Bertwoin waited to hear about this weakness, the alchemist shrugged. "More likely, we are on a fool's quest."

They walked for a while in silence. Bertwoin smiled up at the half-moon. "You are straying from reason and logic, aren't you?"

The master chuckled. "Yes, I'm relying on my experience now, or so I tell myself. I can only hope that I have interpreted Prior Simon's guilt correctly."

Bertwoin glanced at the moonlit Aude. The cruel loss of Emeline for no good reason pressed like a gravestone on his chest, so heavy it threatened to snatch away his breath.

To distract himself, he asked about the other drowning, "Did they ever find Janus's body?"

"No, though Janus may receive justice yet."

"From a *bayle* who chooses not to do anything to find a killer?"

The master held up a hand. "From a *bayle* who was punished by hives and diarrhea. Not wanting to stay on the angry side of God or Na Thea, he arrested Guillaume for killing Janus. He has not yet named the witness, but I hear he claims it is a man of sound character."

They quieted as they approached the abbey, its white-washed walls gleaming like expensive white marble in the moonlight. As they came nearer, they heard the murmur of men's voices praising God and His works.

"Let's hope," the alchemist said, "they continue long enough to give us the time we need."

Bertwoin led the way to a small side door known as the beggar's door and squeaked it open. The monks' sonorous chanting became louder.

Once inside, the master told him, "We need to visit the *dortoir* on the other side, not the dormitory for the lay brothers."

Bertwoin wondered how the master would react if he learned that Flowia and he had hidden in a storeroom attic within these walls. And how would he react if he knew they were lovers?

He led the way, walking on the grassy strip between the inner buildings and the outer walls. They entered the *dortoir* through a back door at the top of six stone steps.

The hallway was dark, but wan moonlight beamed through tall, narrow windows at either end. Heavy doors lined the walls on both sides.

"Where's the main entrance?" the alchemist whispered.

"In the middle, the dark part."

"Nigellus's cell will be the third on the right from it."

Running his fingers down a wall, Bertwoin led the way to the main doors. They then backtracked to the third door and pushed it open.

Since monks were not allowed to have personal effects, Bertwoin asked, "How can we be certain this cell belongs to Brother Nigellus?"

"We can't. All cells are meant to be anonymous."

The narrow room had a single window with its shutter open and was bare except for a rude bed with a wooden cross hanging on the wall above it.

The alchemist searched under the bed's straw mattress, examined the mattress itself, then walked about, gazing down at the stone floor while Bertwoin watched the murky hall from the open doorway. "What are you looking for?"

"Souvenirs. And there don't seem to be any here."

"Oh, you mean like Emeline's tunic?"

"And maybe the star she wore, or Roqua's tunic. Stolen crosses would also be helpful."

"My father knew a crusader who cut an ear off of all those he killed. Said it helped him remember his victories over them." He glanced around the cell. "But I don't see any place to hide any keepsakes."

The alchemist nodded. "There's nothing secreted in the mattress, and the floor has no loose stones."

"Maybe Nigellus hid them somewhere else. The rooms are inspected."

"True. But I think the murderer will want to keep his souvenirs close so he can fondle them often." The alchemist shuffled to the open doorway. "The next cell down should belong to Brother Gregorius. Let's try our luck there."

It matched Brother Nigellus's room exactly.

Again Bertwoin stood in the doorway, watching the empty hall and listening to the monks. The chanting stopped.

"Master, they've finished praying."

The alchemist raised his head, his long face grave and stark in the weak light, and nodded. He held one end of the straw mattress up with one hand, his other hand hidden inside a slit on its underside. He pulled out part of a tunic, and his face contorted with hatred.

"That bastard," Bertwoin muttered and clenched his hands into fists. "How could the chamberlain not have found these things? There's nothing in here to inspect except the mattress."

"Why bother to inspect a saint?" the alchemist growled. He felt around inside the straw mattress. "There is at least one other tunic here. I can't feel any jewelry, but it probably has fallen to the bottom."

He laid the mattress back in its place. "We'll leave everything here as evidence against him."

A hint of candlelight shone at the main entrance and grew steadily in strength. Bertwoin stepped backward into the cell and closed its door.

"*Sancta Maria*," he whispered. "Our purpose here is not sinful. Let it be only one monk and let him go to his room."

CHAPTER XXVI.

F lowia sat at her kitchen table, drinking ale, enjoying the quiet comfort of being in her home among familiar things and smells. Once they found this killer, she would have Bertwoin cut fresh rushes for her.

Thinking of Bertwoin brought her instant joy. Some judged him as foolish and overly generous, but what daughter would not want him as her father? What wife would not want him as her husband? She yearned for his gentle touch and—

The front door banged open. Startled, she turned, smiling to welcome Bertwoin and the master. Why had they come back instead of going to the abbey?

Brother Gregorius loomed in the doorway, glaring at her like an angry scarecrow, his pallid face lacerated by scratches or self-inflicted cuts. His expression contorted into a grimace of hatred.

She shivered. So it was Gregorius—he was the sick monk, the shadowy killer. And she was alone with him.

He shambled into the front room, leaving the door open. Seeing the unicorn tapestry, he snatched it off the wall and threw on the floor. "Devil's work," he muttered.

Flowia pulled her dagger from the sheath hanging on her belt. No other monks were behind him. Of course, he would be alone. How had he known that Bertwoin and the master were elsewhere? Had he watched their house, or had the Devil just given him luck?

"So it was you, false saint," she hissed. Fear constricted her throat, turning her voice into a high, thin whine. "You're the rabid wolf that kills its own kind."

He pointed at her black robe. "Blasphemous witch. You think to mock us."

"This woman won't be an easy kill for you, demon."

"Mary Magdalene would never come to a blasphemer like you."

So Roqua had told Brother Nigellus her lie, and he had told it to this demented monk. "And no visions have ever come to you, deceiver." Good, her voice now sounded strong and more confident. "You pretended to be too sick to attend night services," she said with contempt. "To serve Satan, your true master, you had to neglect God."

He shuffled a step toward her.

She retreated to the kitchen bench and shoved it against the table, leaving a narrow space between it and the stone wall. She then backed into this long gap and waited, trembling, ready to stab Gregorius. With the bench to her right and the wall on her left, the monk had to come straight into her knife thrusts. She would gut him like a fish.

Talk...she must make this sick monster talk. She must delay his attack as long as possible. Bertwoin and the master might return.

"Why kill young women?" she asked.

Brother Gregorius, his face smug with righteous determination, smiled at her. He snatched up a three-legged stool and threw it at her head. She ducked, and it bounced off the wall behind her.

He crept toward her, his intense eyes on the knife. She backed up and readied for his charge. He snatched up one end of the bench and, with demonic strength, tossed it over the table as if it were no heavier than a straw mattress.

Gregorius grinned, clearly enjoying her fear. "Whore of Babylon," he crooned. "God will punish you."

"Burn in Hell, you twisted fiend," she growled. "You're not God."

Retreating another two steps, Flowia's heel caught on the stool, and she tumbled backward onto the floor.

Gregorius charged forward. He kicked the stool between them so hard it flew over her head and hit the back wall. She rose to her knees. He rushed in and grabbed her coif and the hair coiled under it.

She stabbed at his groin with her knife. Shock trembled up her arm as the blade missed his groin but sank deep into the flesh of his thigh and struck bone. He screamed and shrank away from her, his movement jerking the dagger out of her hand.

They both stared, paralyzed. The knife protruded from his thigh, pinning the black robe to his wounded leg. Flowia recovered from her shock and lunged for the dagger's handle. He slapped her hand aside.

Eyes flaring, Gregorius clutched the knife's hilt with both hands. He screamed as he ripped the blade free from his flesh.

How could she fight this monster? How could she save herself? The excruciating pain from his wounded leg should have crippled him. Any other man would have collapsed. But not this relentless hellion: he thrived on self-mutilation and pain.

She must get to the door. She must reach the forest and hide.

She shoved a hand against the rushes, pushing herself up,

twisting as she did so, and leaped to her feet. As she stumbled away from the Devil-possessed monk, she looked frantically for something, anything, to use as a weapon.

She was jerked backward. He had grabbed her cowl. She turned and punched his face. He flinched but didn't let go of her cowl. Their eyes met. No human pity showed in his. She clawed at his face, reopening some of his wounds while he tried to slap her hands away and grab her.

As they wrestled, they smacked against the kitchen table. A jug rolled off and fell on the rushes. The taper she had glued to the table with melted wax toppled and, like the jug, rolled off. Instinctively, Flowia dropped to her knees, ripping her cowl out of his hand. She slapped out the flame before it caught the rushes on fire.

Quick as a ferret, Brother Gregorius slipped behind her, grabbed her around the waist, and lifted her off the ground. He purred, "Fire! Yes, fire. Now you shall burn, witch."

She kicked backward, her heel slamming against his injured thigh. He huffed in pain and let go of her. She scrambled away on her hands and knees.

She bumped against a bucket of water and knocked it over. She saw him snatch the fallen jug off the rushes. Rising, she lurched to her feet and started to run for the front door.

Blinding pain slammed the back of her head. Lightning burst behind her eyes, and her body went rigid with breathless shock, and she tumbled into a dark abyss.

CHAPTER XXVII.

Bertwoin pressed his ear to the door and listened for the brother to go to his cell. Since monks were denied privacy, none of the doors had locks on them.

The footsteps moved closer, paused, then their door smacked inward against his head. With his fist raised, Bertwoin stepped aside to let Brother Gregorius enter. Candlelight blinded him.

"What?" a monk barked. "Bertwoin?" Then in an even more surprised tone, the monk whispered, "And the alchemist?"

Bertwoin's eyesight cleared enough for him to recognize Brother Theodoric. He lowered his fist.

The pudgy little monk stood stricken and scared with a hand raised to protect himself.

"I didn't kill her," Bertwoin said. "I would never harm Emeline."

Brother Theodoric frowned. Then he nodded, though he moved half a step away from Bertwoin. "Prior Simon says it wasn't you." He raised his candle to light the room. "What have you done with Brother Gregorius?"

"He's not here. We were looking for him."

Brother Theodoric held up a small clay jar. "I came to check on his condition and apply a salve." He shook his head and asked Bertwoin, "But why would you be in the *dortoir*? It's outrageous. Everyone in the abbey is looking for you." He reared to full height. "And how dare you wear a habit?"

"Wasn't he at matins?" the master interrupted in a hoarse whisper.

"No, he's mutilated himself again." Brother Theodoric frowned at the empty bed.

"He didn't attend prayers?" the alchemist asked, now clearly alarmed.

"Leave now," Brother Theodoric ordered, stepping back so they could go past him. "You don't belong here. If I find you here again, I will inform the abbot."

Without arguing, they slipped past him and ran down the dim hallway to the side door they had used to enter the building. Bertwoin peeked outside, saw no monks, and rushed down the six steps with the master at his heels. They circled the inner buildings to the beggar's door. Bertwoin opened it and sighed with relief when they stepped outside.

The master grabbed his arm. "Flowia is alone at home. I'll follow you. Run, Bertwoin, run faster than lightning."

WHEN BERTWOIN REACHED THE PLAITED MULBERRY HEDGE, he was surprised to see the front door of the master's cottage gaping open. A tremor rippled up his backbone. Had Brother Gregorius taken her? Or had she escaped?

Fearing what he might see, Bertwoin crept to the doorway. There was enough light from the dying hearth fire for him to see that no one was in the front room or in the kitchen where the furniture was thrown about.

Please let it be that she escaped.

Bertwoin took a few deep breaths to calm his thoughts and his thumping heart. Maybe someone else had come for her, someone who needed her to nurse them. No, that was stupid. Everyone knew she had gone into hiding when he did.

He shook his head to clear it and settle his roiling thoughts. He must stay focused. He crossed himself and slipped his knife out of its leather sheath.

He sprang into the front room, hoping his sudden charge would surprise anyone waiting in ambush. Nothing moved. He checked the bedrooms...empty. He climbed partway up the ladder and peered into the dark *solier*...also empty.

Everything in the kitchen was a jumble. She had fought him. Bertwoin saw a candle lying on the floor rushes and picked it up. He felt the taper's wick...completely cold. He moved the table aside and, getting down on his knees, he blew the hearth embers back into flame.

How would he live without her?

Bertwoin prowled the disorderly kitchen, looking for clues, as the master would have done. Why had they left her alone? The air hung heavy with the sour smell of old rushes and a hint of burned tallow. A jug lay broken on the tousled rushes. The bucket of water he had brought her from the spring lay on its side.

He saw her knife lying on the floor. Part of its blade was darker than its hilt. He picked it up and sniffed the blade. Was it the killer's blood or hers?

Please let it be his. Please.

The cold candlewick meant that Gregorius, if he wasn't seriously wounded, had a comfortable head start on him. Despite forcing himself to breathe slowly, his heart pounded, and he felt as if he might retch. His frantic thoughts threatened to fly beyond his control.

As he stepped through the front doorway, he noticed a

dark streak not halfway up the doorframe. Bertwoin swiped the spot with a forefinger, smelled it, tasted it, and winced. Was it Flowia's blood or the monk's?

He began to run to save a life as precious as his own.

CHAPTER XXVIII.

Bertwoin sprinted straight toward the ghost-ridden Devil's Doorstep and its brooding Gallows Oak. If a demon dropped out of the hanging tree and blocked his way, well, he would call upon God for help and trust in the speed of his legs.

He skimmed along at a ground-swallowing pace. With luck, he would come upon the insane brother and Flowia before they reached the pit. Her candle had been cold, but dragging or carrying her might slow Gregorius down, especially if she had wounded him.

Was he willing to kill a monk and become an outlaw for life? The Church would excommunicate him, and his soul would be at risk. Yes, he would send the pitiless brother to Hell, especially if he had harmed Flowia. Only he could give Emeline and Roqua the justice they deserved.

A shadowy figure appeared on the path in front of him. He stuttered a step, saw that it was a person, not a demon, and charged. As he slammed his lowered right shoulder into the man, he saw Agbart's mouth open in surprise. The woodcutter yelped and sprawled backward.

Bertwoin raced away, confident the woodcutter was not fleet enough to catch him, yet hoping that Agbart would follow him and help capture the mad monk.

As Bertwoin neared the Devil's Doorstep, he slowed to a trot so as not to run full speed into a demon's arms. The solemn Gallows Oak came into sight around the bend.

No corpses dangled from its ponderous limbs. Bertwoin signed a cross to celebrate this blessing. Then he drew his dagger and sprinted under the oak's weighty branches.

Not far down the path, he dodged into the dark shrubbery under trees that trembled in the light wind. Bertwoin picked his way over roots and fallen limbs and tried to move as quietly as an owl in flight so he would catch the monk by surprise.

Near the linden grove, a fire's faint glow rose out of the ground. Hope sank in his chest like a stone in water.

Bertwoin charged forward, ignoring the branches and twigs that slapped his face. He stumbled over a tree root but somehow kept his balance and staggered into the grove of linden trees. He swerved around the rock formation at the front of the broad pit and half-ran, half-slid down the sloping backside.

Brother Gregorius hunched like a ghoul over a small fire off to one side of the kingly linden tree dominating the enclosure's center. He studied Bertwoin for a breath or two, then shrugged and ignored him. Stunned, Bertwoin watched him feed a handful of twigs into his blaze.

Flowia stood erect, wearing only her gray linen chemise, with her spine pressed against the linden's trunk. She was gagged, with her arms stretched behind her. The gray bark around her was scorched black from previous fires.

Gregorius had thrown kindling and branches around Flowia's feet, covering the bottom of her linen chemise up to her shins. Larger pieces of wood for his witch-burning blaze lay stacked two steps away from her.

She gazed at Bertwoin as if a winged angel had appeared in answer to her pleading prayers.

"I'm here," he blurted out. Relief that she wasn't badly hurt lifted his spirits and confidence.

Gregorius continued to shove branches into his small fire with the self-satisfied smile of someone doing holy work, his movements calm and precise. Bertwoin's sudden intrusion into the pit seemed of little concern to him.

Scratches had bled recently on his left cheek. So, Flowia had fought him with her fingernails. Bertwoin didn't doubt that Emeline had also scratched the monk's reptilian face. Gregorius had added martyrdom cuts of his own to cover her telling marks.

The monk studied Bertwoin's black habit, his expression serene. The wavering firelight whitewashed his face, darkening the scratches on his forehead and cheeks so they seemed bone-deep.

"You'll not save the witch, peasant." He showed no more feeling than if he were weeding Brother Theodoric's garden or boiling beans for supper.

"You're a false saint," Bertwoin growled. "A liar. You don't have visions."

"Neither does she. And though she attends mass, she is not a true daughter of the Church." Smiling, Gregorius gazed up at the half-moon. "Visions will come to me after I have rid our diocese of vermin like her. Even the holy Pope will agree."

Did he really think he would come to the Pope's attention? Flowia had thrown him bait he couldn't ignore when she'd claimed to have had a saintly vision. Gregorius would not tolerate competition.

Bertwoin took a step toward the monk. "You killed two women, you depraved bastard. You'll not do it a third time."

The brother grinned. "I already have."

Bertwoin shivered. So he had killed poor Brune. "Tell me, monk, how did you find Flowia?"

Brother Gregorius giggled. "You already know that."

"Do I?"

"Did you think I didn't know to watch the alchemist's house? The old pagan can't do without his virgin. And Saint Nazarius smoothed my path by sending you and the wicked alchemist away. This was a sign that he blessed my work and that tonight was the night."

Bertwoin muttered. "How can you believe in the Virgin Mary yet torture gentle girls like Emeline and Roqua and Brune?"

"What does a peasant know?" Gregorius sneered. "Only pain wipes away sin. The Lord showed us that. And fire purifies the flesh." He pointed a bony finger at Bertwoin's face and quoted with sanctimonious fervor, "'Thou shalt not suffer a witch to live.'"

"She's not a witch or a heretic," Bertwoin shouted.

"Of course she is. Her skin is the color of a chestnut. She knows the ways of plants. She's the alchemist's virgin."

Bertwoin watched the monk bend and pick up twigs for his little blaze. How long would it take for the master to reach his empty house, see the damage done there, and hurry to this forest pit? And where was Agbart? Why had the woodcutter not yet found them?

Flowia watched him with a disappointed and questioning look. He turned his face away. She wanted him to untie her. But he sensed that this duty-crazed saint would fight him with the fury and strength of a fiend. It would be safer once the master and Agbart arrived.

"Who are you to judge them as witches, monk? Emeline was more devout than you'll ever be. You drowned one more blameless than you."

"Burn them or drown them, either death is a fitting end for a Godless witch." Gregorius limped towards Flowia. He watched Bertwoin, her would-be savior, with a sly amused expression.

Brother Gregorius pulled out his knife. "It is time for the alchemist's virgin to suffer. Her life is lost, but her immortal soul may yet be saved." He pulled a silver cross hanging on a chain around his neck from under his black robe. "The rood and this," he said as he raised his knife, "are the tools needed to purify her soul."

Gregorius glanced at Bertwoin's undrawn knife and shoved his dagger back into the sheath on his rope belt.

"I shall not defile my blade with your peasant blood. It must be kept pure for her." He jerked a thumb at Flowia behind him. "And I don't need it to defeat a mere peasant, not when Saint Nazarius stands with me."

Without warning, Bertwoin charged the monk, dropping his shoulder to slam him off his feet. Laughing, Gregorius stepped into his attack, twisted, and flipped him over one hip. Bertwoin thudded to the ground flat on his back, his breath huffing out of him, and his injured ribs stabbing pain into his chest.

Gregorius tottered sideways with his hands clasped over leg wound.

Bertwoin rolled, rising to his knees. He cried out and arched backwards when Gregorius kicked his spine with a leather sandal, and a ball of pain rolled up his spine.

Gritting his teeth, Bertwoin feinted left, dodged right, then staggered to standing. He faced the brother, who watched him with calm curiosity. Had Gregorius trained for the knighthood before deciding to join the Church?

How could the wounded monk be so agile? How could he stand the pain?

They both pounced, smacking against each other, clawing

for a hold. Again the monk threw Bertwoin over his hip. Before Bertwoin could rise to his feet, Gregorius dropped on his upper back, slamming his mouth against the stony ground. He then knelt on Bertwoin and pounded his jaw twice with a fist. Stars swirled in front of Bertwoin's eyes.

Lurching sideways, he toppled Gregorius off of him. Grappling, they rolled over and over across the rocky soil, each trying to end up on top. Bertwoin tumbled into the monk's stinging fire and screeched. He flung Gregorius from him and rolled across the rocky ground, beating at sparks sizzling on his black habit. Then he sat up, his vision still hazy from the blows the monk had given him.

Gregorius locked an elbow across Bertwoin's Adam's apple. Bertwoin punched upward over his head and smacked Gregorius's face. The monk squawked and fell backward. Bertwoin whirled and threw himself on top of him.

They wrestled, grunting and cursing, and Gregorius somehow slithered out from under him. They both climbed to their knees, gasping with pain. Gregorius punched Bertwoin twice, yelling with each blow. Again Bertwoin saw comets swirl before his eyes. How could he bring this bastard down?

They scrabbled at each other, neither able to rise and stand. Bertwoin grabbed the monk's ears, jerked the snarling face toward him, and smashed his forehead against Gregorius's nose. Blood spurted from the nostrils.

Gregorius clung to Bertwoin's right arm with furious desperation and like a snake sank his teeth into Bertwoin's knuckles. Bertwoin screamed. With superhuman effort, he again tossed the monk aside, then clasped his injured hand against his chest and rocked back and forth to relieve the stinging ache.

Gregorius lumbered to his feet and again slipped behind Bertwoin while he was still on his knees. He wrapped an arm around Bertwoin's throat and squeezed. Bertwoin couldn't breathe. He staggered to his feet, dragging Gregorius up with him, though this intensified the pressure on his throat, and still he couldn't break the monk's deadly stranglehold.

He shoved Gregorius backward, gaining speed as he went, and slammed him into the basin's rock wall. Both of them went down and stayed down, gasping for sweet air.

Bertwoin climbed to his knees. He must get up, must rise before the monk did. But his body was tired and slow to react.

Gregorius staggered up and yelled, "Peasant," as if it were a curse. He seized Bertwoin's ankle and began dragging him, face down, to his small fire. Bertwoin flipped over, grabbed Gregorius's robe, and pulled him down on top of him. The monk sat on his chest and began to choke him.

Bertwoin clawed at the hands clamped on his throat but couldn't loosen them. He saw the slit in Gregorius's robe where the wool was stiff with blood and slammed the butt of his fist down on the monk's injured thigh.

Gregorius screeched and jittered. Bertwoin tried to shove the monk to one side, but Gregorius, mewling with pain, stayed on Bertwoin's chest and again grabbed his throat with both hands.

Then the crazed monk's head jerked forward, and he slowly tumbled off Bertwoin and lay still.

The master stood behind Gregorius's sprawled body with a weighty fire log in one hand. He looked down into Bertwoin's eyes with an expression of profound sorrow.

Bertwoin lurched to his feet, then stumbled sideways. The master rushed forward to hold him upright. The pit swirled around Bertwoin. Despite the master's help, he fell again to his aching knees and curled forward with his brow pressed against the hard ground.

The alchemist patted Bertwoin's back. "Just rest here a

moment, young plowman. You've done your work. Oh, how you've done your work."

Bertwoin groaned, too weak to move. Even his eyelids hurt. After a few breaths, tender hands stroked his hair.

"How will we ever get him home?" Flowia asked.

Bertwoin realized the master had cut her loose. He took a deep breath and sat up. Flowia gasped and stared at his face with her hands pressed against her cheeks. Sudden tears glistened in her eyes.

He smiled to reassure her and said, "I'm a Teisseire. I'll heal."

With the master's and Flowia's help, he rose. The effort made him pant as if he had just finished a footrace.

"We need to get him to our house so I can tend to his wounds," Flowia said.

"We will tie the monk to a tree," the master murmured. "And don't forget to tend to your own wounds, daughter."

She stared at the welts on her wrists. "They sting, but a salve will do for them."

Agbart charged down the sloping rear of the pit into the enclosure's circle of firelight. They all stared at him. His hair resembled brambles, his tunic was filthy, and his forehead was bruised where he had probably beaten it against a chapel's stone floor in lamentation.

The woodcutter snarled at Bertwoin. "I followed you, hell's meat. I spied your fire and knew God had answered my prayers."

"I seem to have found your murderer for you, woodcutter," the master said.

"And I aim to pay you, as agreed." He eyed Bertwoin with merciless fury.

"Not him," Flowia said.

"What?" Confused, Agbart frowned at her.

Flowia jabbed her forefinger at the unconscious monk

lying at their feet. "*He* judged your Emeline as a heretic. *He* tried to burn her."

Agbart stared red-eyed and unbelieving down at Brother Gregorius.

Flowia shuddered and folded herself against Bertwoin's chest. He hugged her quivering body and patted her back and saw that her touching him, more than her words, convinced Agbart of his innocence.

"Brother Gregorius felt it his duty to rid Carcassonne and our diocese of heretics," Flowia said, her voice muffled by Bertwoin's woolen robe.

Agbart trembled in an ague of grief. He made a choking sound, then with tears flowing down his dirty cheeks, he looked at the master for confirmation.

"It's true, woodcutter. The monk burned and drowned your daughter."

Agbart grunted. He strode to Gregorius, grabbed his loose cowl like a cat picking up a kitten, lifted him, and hoisted him over one shoulder.

"Agbart," said Flowia, stepping away from Bertwoin, her spine now as straight as a fletcher's ash-wood arrow. "He wants martyrdom. Why give it to him? Think of your own soul."

The woodcutter's face turned ferocious. "The Church court will protect him. They'll say God meant for him to kill my girl because of her beliefs."

Agbart bounced Gregorius on his shoulder, adjusting the monk's weight as if he were nothing more than a sack of barley flour. "He wants to be a martyr. Well, maybe God wants that too. Otherwise, why deliver him into my hands?"

The sturdy woodcutter marched up the sloping side of the torture pit and disappeared into the night.

CHAPTER XXIX.

Bertwoin woke as if falling out of a dark sky and found himself naked in an unknown room. Then he remembered fighting Brother Gregorius and how he had come to lie on this straw mattress in Flowia's bedroom.

He rolled onto his side and winced when pain stabbed his ribs. Every nerve in his body felt as if pricked by a dagger's point. Groaning, he sat up.

Flowia bustled into the room. "Thought I heard a pig grunt in here," she chirped in contrast to her sympathetic expression.

"I feel like I've just been born," he answered in a voice still husky from Gregorius's chokehold.

"You look like it too."

"Now I know what Hell is going to feel like."

"You've been delirious for three days."

"*Three* days?"

"Mumbling and flailing about. Sweated the whole time. Kept your clothes sopping wet, so we just took them off of you."

Flowia had traded her black monk's robe for an ankle-length green dress and had gathered her long black hair behind her head in a white linen coif. Bertwoin assumed this meant she didn't expect to return to the abbey's storeroom attic.

"So no one came to arrest us?"

"The master has been busy on that score. He went to the *château* to speak on our behalf, and our story pleased the *visconte's* noble ear. The *bayle* was also pleased to believe that Brother Gregorius was the murderer. He didn't have to arrest you and make your formidable father his enemy."

She squatted down beside him and, lifting his left hand, began to unwind the linen strip binding it. His knuckles were still yellow and blue, but the bite wound was scabbed over.

"It's healing well," she told him. "You don't need the bandage anymore."

"So the *bayle* is happy?"

"Like a terrier with a rat. He's also in a gladsome mood because Bishop Othon took custody of Guillaume and said he would oversee the interrogations. So the *bayle* need not torture Guillaume and need not incur the wrath of the drowned-finder's sons."

She kissed his injured hand. "And I'm told your father stopped hiring out his mules. No more pulling carts now for Left and Right. He's resting them for the plowing season."

She grinned when he groaned.

> *"There is no rest for heroes, it seems*
> *because fathers expect them to plow more seams.*
> *Clanoud has doubled his usual price*
> *because fame makes furrow cutting more precise."*

"Who told you all this?" he asked.

"Your mother. She comes every day. She'll be happy not to see you thrashing about feverishly on my bed."

"Well, my father will just have to rest me like our plow mules. I want time to heal."

"Let's hope he agrees."

"I already fought one crazy man and held my own. I can do it again, especially since he has to be careful not to injure me overly much. I have to be able-bodied to plow furrows."

Flowia lifted a finger for his attention. "By the way, I fetched Michel's seedlings from the forest and transplanted them in my medicine garden. It's easier to tend them here."

"Michel will not be happy about you owning his plants," Bertwoin warned. "He expected to see some profit from them."

"I'll cross that river when I reach it. I've helped his family twice. And remember, he *stole* them." She shrugged. "I might locate a denier or two for him."

Flowia stood up. "The master is in his workshop. He'll want to see you once you get up. But first, you need to eat."

"I need water. My throat is a desert."

Bertwoin painfully slipped into his chemise and black monk's habit before eating and drinking his fill. Then he shuffled to the workshop behind Flowia, who carried a pitcher of sour wine and slices of goat cheese on a birch platter.

Sitting beside his brick oven, the alchemist inspected Bertwoin, then waved at a stool near him. "So the young hero is up and about again."

Flowia placed the platter and the pitcher on a small table within the master's reach. "He's weak as a worm, but all his parts seem to work, including his stomach."

The alchemist smiled at Bertwoin. "Our young *visconte* is pleased with both of you. I told him it was Flowia's plan that plucked you from the bishop's dungeon. He thought it a saucy joke to use fake monks to snatch you away from a churchman."

The master nodded at Flowia's throat. "It was the *visconte* who gave her the pendant she now wears. I could never afford so pricey a gem."

Flowia pulled a silver chain out of the neck of her dress with a teardrop pendant hung from it, its stone greenish-blue. She dangled the gem in front of Bertwoin.

The master smiled. "It is called jade and blesses whoever wears it. I am informed that when it is tapped by the gem-cutter's hammer, it rings like the melodious voice of a lover."

Blushing and suddenly shy, Flowia glanced at Bertwoin. She fingered the pendant as if to convince herself that it was real. Bertwoin wished *he* could give her something so nice.

"And to show the *visconte's* further approval," the master said to Bertwoin, "he gave me a dagger with an ash handle. It lies waiting for you in my bedroom. Suffice it to say that your friends will envy you the owning of it."

Bertwoin shook his head. "My father will take it from me or have me sell it and take most of the money."

The master stared up at the roof's shingles as he considered the problem. Then he smiled. "Tell him the *visconte* will take that as an insult. He will think you did not treasure his gift."

Bertwoin laughed. "I'll feel the brunt of that."

"But heroes," Flowia said, looking at him with pride, "can take punishment."

Bertwoin sat up a bit straighter. "They can. And they fight tyrants, no matter *who* they are."

The master rubbed his hands together. "Yes, Flowia gave me a detailed account of your battle against Brother Gregorius. People at the market would have paid a rich man's harvest to see such a battle."

Bertwoin touched his sore throat. "I think Brother Gregorius trained to be one who fights before he decided to become one who prays."

"As is often the case with extra noble sons," the alchemist muttered.

Bertwoin leaned forward on his stool and stretched his aching back. "And you've also had no trouble from Bishop Othon or Abbot Jehan?"

"They pretend to be ignorant of everything. May God punish them both." The goldsmith chopped the edge of one hand against the palm of the other. "They officially ignore the evidence, and the Devil has given them the wiles to do so."

"Evidence? You mean the tunics hidden in Brother Gregorius's mattress?"

The master nodded. "I let Prior Simon know what we had found. He sent two monks he trusted to clean Brother Gregorius's cell, supposedly to ready it for the next occupant, since the saintly Gregorius has disappeared."

"And every woman in the diocese already knows," Flowia interrupted, "that Agbart carried him away and chopped him into flesh-and-bone kindling."

"As does the *bayle*," the alchemist added. When he saw Bertwoin's stricken look, he patted the air to calm him. "No, he has not arrested Agbart, nor does he need to. The woodcutter had Gertrude give him the *consolamentum,* the last sacrament. So now he lies starving himself to death, convinced that in doing so his soul will fly off to the good god.

The master continued, "Prior Simon's two monks found three tunics hidden inside Brother Gregorius's bedstraw mattress and a number of stolen crosses. Though Gregorius is now dead, Bishop Othon and Abbot Jehan toil hard to fool us into thinking he is still the golden monk."

The alchemist set a small iron frame on his squat brick oven and laid a flat piece of iron with holes in it across the frame's top.

"Though the abbot ignores the damning evidence against

saintly Brother Gregorius," the alchemist said as he worked, "he hasn't ignored the two monks who told others about finding the three tunics. The abbot ordered the brothers to fast for a week, to keep silent for a month, and sentenced them both to the demeaning duty of cleaning the abbey's privy chambers for three months. He has hurled his fury against them."

The old master lit two stubby candles and slid them inside the frame. Then he set a glass beaker with measurement markings up one side on the flat top above the candle flames. He pointed to a greenish corked bottle, and Flowia handed it to him.

The master said to Bertwoin, "Prior Simon accepts Brother Gregorius's guilt, of course. He was the demented monk's confessor. He insists that the abbey monks pray for Brother Gregorius's soul. It is rumored also that he is lenient with the two monks who found the evidence. Perhaps that is because he ordered these two brothers to find the tunics."

The alchemist unstoppered the green bottle and poured clear liquid up to the lowest mark in the glass, letting it heat while they talked.

"And to think," Bertwoin mumbled, "I thought Prior Simon might actually be Emeline's killer."

"You did recognize his guilt," the alchemist praised. "But it was the guilt of one who knows the secret of a depraved murderer yet cannot break the seal of confession. He was relieved when I told him we had found those tunics."

The alchemist clapped his thin hands. "Ah well, the bishop is off to Rome for six months, no doubt to consider matters more serious to him than the murders of three peasant women. I think he intends to forget about the lowly plowman, sometimes called Ox, who escaped from his mighty dungeon."

Bertwoin stared morosely at his bruised knuckles. "So

now, he has given my trial and punishment over to Abbot Jehan."

"Ah, yes, assaulting a monk and trespass. Serious offenses indeed."

The liquid in the beaker quickly heated to a bubbling simmer. Seeing this, the alchemist paused to pick up a foreign coin and scrub it until its copper shone.

Flowia glanced at the master and said, "But again the Devil has given you luck, Brother Bertwoin. The good abbot suffered a mysterious and humbling bout of food poisoning after eating a sumptuous dinner. As he lay in his bed, preparing to die, Prior Simon convinced him to forgive you for your trespasses against the abbey. Within two days, Abbot Jehan recovered. Forgiveness has wondrous powers."

"How did you—?"

"Do you think you are the only one who can slip into the abbey without being seen?"

He marveled at her courage. "What if you had been caught?"

"But I wasn't."

The alchemist flicked a pinch of gray crystals into the simmering liquid and dropped in the reddish-brown coin. "It was foolish of her to visit the abbey," he said, glaring at her.

"Yes," Bertwoin agreed. "What were you thinking?"

Flowia stared down her nose at him.

He smiled up at her. "And have they forgiven you for the sin of defying Church authority and rescuing me?"

"What sin?" she asked as if shocked that he could believe she deserved punishment. "I and the false monks were just players in the plowman's clever plot to escape. Though the *visconte* knows the plan was mine, the clerics do not. So I am not important enough to merit their punishment."

"Your father will be proud of you," the master told Bertwoin.

"He'll say it only shows what good fathering will do."

They all laughed. The alchemist picked the coin out of the simmering liquid with a slender pair of tongs and held it up.

Bertwoin exclaimed, "That's magic."

"Yes, nature's magic," the master said. "So now it looks silver. Let's see if we can't turn it golden."

The master picked up a scrap of hemp cloth to protect his hand and set the hot glass beaker on his brick oven to cool. Using the tongs, he dropped the silver coin on the hot top over the frame and let it sizzle above the candle flames.

Bertwoin cleared his throat. "Even if Abbot Jehan has forgiven me, Bishop Othon might remember I tweaked his nose."

"Ah," the master said with a wink, "but I share the seneschal's opinion on that. The bishop will forget Bertwoin was ever a guest under his palace. He doesn't want to remind everyone from beggar to nobleman of his failure to keep a simple plowman in his dungeon. And who knows, wily Bertwoin might escape a second time." Well pleased, the smiling alchemist picked a slice of goat cheese off the platter on the small table and bit into it.

Bertwoin eyed Flowia as he asked the master, "Did you not tell me when we talked of Janus, that like the abbot, the *bayle* also suffered from food poisoning?"

"That wasn't me," she protested. "Na Thea dosed the lawman's soup or ale. Everyone knew he was letting Guillaume run free after drowning her brother."

The master chuckled. He and Flowia glanced at each other with knowing smiles.

"And there is a rumor about Janus too," Flowia gloated. "A carter says he saw Janus downriver in the Trebes area. Calls himself Ouen now. And Ouen says Janus drowned as prophesied. The man we knew is now someone else."

"So Janus sidestepped his fate. But doesn't that mean that if the *bayle* or Guillaume's sons find him, Guillaume need not hang for drowning him?"

"Ah well, we haven't told you everything yet," the alchemist said. He used the small tongs to pick up the hot coin and held it up in front of Bertwoin. It had turned golden.

"You did it," Bertwoin shouted.

"Not really," the alchemist said, shaking his head. "Like Saint Gregorius, it only seems golden."

The master blew out the candle flames. He looked up at Flowia, nodded, and waited.

No longer smiling, she stared down into Bertwoin's face. "While torturing a confession out of Guillaume for drowning Janus, the bishop also extracted one from him for killing Emeline, Roqua, and Brune."

Bertwoin made a disgusted sound in his throat. "So Agbart was right. The Church protected their saint. They do so even after his death."

"Yes, Brother Gregorius is now proved innocent." Flowia bowed her head in resignation. "Maybe Gertrude and the Good Folk *are* right. Earth is the evil god's domain."

"Even so," the master said, "the burning of young women here has stopped for now."

Did you enjoy The Plowman's Plight? If so, please leave a review and tell your friends. Bertwoin and Flowia's adventures will continue in *The Wrathful Cup of Scorn.*

ABOUT THE AUTHOR

E. A. RIVIÈRE lives in a magical forest where mice claiming to be cousins move in for the winter then take the towels when they leave in spring. He is a winner in the Writers of the Future contest, a graduate of the six-week Odyssey Fantasy Writing Workshop, and a grand prize winner of the Sidney Lanier Poetry Competition.

His paranormal mysteries **Magic and Murder Among the Dwarves** and **The Dwarf Assassin** are available on Amazon under the author name Erik Bundy.

Unlike many writers, he doesn't keep a cat in deference to his mouse cousins and because he couldn't live up to its expectations.

ACKNOWLEDGMENTS

Appreciation is due to:

Barbara Campbell for professional editing that turned a flawed manuscript into a one readers might like.

Derek Murphy for creating the first exciting cover and for allowing me to join his writing group at a castle in France where I wrote much of this novel.

Dave Pasquantonio for proofreading *The Plowman's Plight* and catching a number of mistakes. He also formatted the manuscript and readied it for publication.

Eleanor Bundy, my beta reader, who kept me from embarrassing myself.